"A MAJOR ARTIST!"
The New York Times Book Review

YEVGENY ZAMYATIN was born in Russia in 1884. A friend of Gorky, Zamyatin was an enthusiastic supporter of the Revolution—at first. *WE*, written in 1921 and 1922, was circulated clandestinely, and even though it was denied publication, *WE* became one of the most influential and talked-about novels of this century. Zamyatin was exiled under Stalin and died in Paris in 1937. His masterpiece remains unpublished in his native Russia.

WE

Yevgeny Zamyatin

Translated by Mirra Ginsburg

AVON BOOKS ◆ NEW YORK

AVON BOOKS
A division of
The Hearst Corporation
105 Madison Avenue
New York, New York 10016

English language copyright © 1972 by Mirra Ginsburg
Front cover illustration by Harold Siegel
Published by arrangement with the author
Library of Congress Catalog Card Number: 83-90620
ISBN: 0-380-63313-2

First Bard Printing: August 1983
First Avon Printing: July 1987

AVON TRADEMARK REG. U.S. PAT. OFF. AND IN OTHER COUNTRIES, MARCA REGISTRADA, HECHO EN U.S.A.

Printed in the U.S.A.

K-R   10 9   8   7   6

We played a fateful role in Yevgeny Zamyatin's life. An epitome of his philosophy, the novel prefigured his own future and that of his country with astonishing accuracy. Zamyatin's credo is best expressed in the words of the heroine of *We*: "There is no final revolution. Revolutions are infinite," and, "I do not want anyone to want for me—I want to want for myself."

These two principles—eternal change, and freedom of the individual to choose, to want, to create according to his own need and his own will—dominated both his life and his work. "We shall break down all walls—to let the green wind blow free from end to end—across the earth," says his heroine. Small wonder he was hated and hounded by those who demanded uniformity and total compliance with an outside will—the state's, the Benefactor's, the Party's.

A powerful and original writer, and an entirely modern one, Zamyatin is deeply rooted in the traditions of Russian literature. He is a direct descendant of Gogol and Dostoyevsky, the favorites of his childhood. He is also close kin to Leskov, Chekhov, Shchedrin, and his own contemporaries Alexey Remizov and Andrey Bely. Like Gogol and Dostoyevsky, he is profoundly concerned with central moral problems; like all of them, he is a great master of satire, style, and the grotesque.

Zamyatin was born in 1884 in Lebedyan, one of the most colorful towns in the heart of the Russian black-earth belt, some two hundred miles southeast of Moscow—a region of fertile fields, of ancient churches and monasteries, of country fairs, gypsies and swindlers, nuns and innkeepers, buxom Russian beauties, and merchants who made and lost millions overnight. It was also a region that preserved a richly expressive folk speech, which Zamyatin absorbed and later used to magnificent effect in many of his stories, plays, and novellas.

His father, an Orthodox priest, taught religion at the local school. His mother was a talented pianist.

A naval engineer by training, Zamyatin early turned to literature. In 1913 he published the novella "A Provincial Tale," and in 1914 "At the World's End," satirizing army life in a remote garrison town. The journal in which the latter appeared was confiscated by the Tsarist authorities, and both the editor and the author were brought to trial for "maligning the Russian officer corps." The charges were dismissed, but this was only one of Zamyatin's lifelong clashes with constituted authority.

As a student at the St. Petersburg Polytechnical Institute during the early years of the century, Zamyatin had joined the Bolshevik faction of the Social-Democratic Party. Arrested during the revolution of 1905, he spent some months in solitary confinement and on his release was exiled from St.

Petersburg. After a short stay in Lebedyan, he came back to the capital, where he lived "illegally" (and even continued his schooling) until 1911, when the police finally caught up with him and exiled him a second time. It was during this exile that he wrote "A Provincial Tale." In 1913 he was amnestied and permitted to reside in St. Petersburg.

On graduation from the Polytechnic Institute, he was invited to serve on its faculty. For some years literature was largely superseded by teaching and engineering work. During World War I, Zamyatin was sent to England to design and supervise the construction of some of the earliest Russian icebreakers. When the Revolution of 1917 broke out, he could not endure to be away from Russia and hastened back, bringing with him two tales satirizing English life, "The Islanders" and "The Fisher of Men."

In Russia, Zamyatin (no longer a Bolshevik) threw himself with tremendous energy into the great cultural and artistic upsurge that followed the revolution. This was a period of fantastic contradictions. Russia lay in ruins after years of war, revolution, and continuing civil strife. Her economic life had all but wholly broken down. Transportation, communication, the food supply, the contact between city and village were in total disarray. Yet in the midst of hunger and cold, a band of dedicated spirits took it upon themselves not only to save the country's culture but to present to the hitherto deprived masses the cultural heritage of the entire world.

Initiated chiefly by Gorky, the veritable patron saint of Russian literature in those grim days, a number of organizations were formed, both to keep writers, scholars, and artists physically alive and to permit them to continue their work. In

Petersburg, these included the House of the Arts, established in 1920 in the unheated former palace of the great merchant Yeliseyev, where writers were given lodgings in every available room and cubbyhole; the House of Scientists; and a number of publishing houses and literary journals (Zamyatin served on the editorial boards of several of these). Studios were organized where young writers were taught the elements of their craft by such writers, poets, and translators as Zamyatin, Gumilyov, Lozinsky, Chukovsky, and others. Both teachers and students often had to cross the frozen city on foot and sit, in unheated rooms, dressed in old coats, sweaters, mufflers, chilled and hungry but totally absorbed in the brilliant discussions of literature.

A variety of schools and movements proliferated in all the arts, some of them continuing with renewed vigor from prewar days, others entirely new. Endless disputes raged between symbolists, futurists, constructivists, formalists, acmeists, imaginists, neo-realists, and, of course, the increasingly powerful and vocal groups of proletarian writers and critics who regarded literature as the mere instrument of the revolution and social change. Zamyatin became the leader and teacher of the Serapion Brethren, a group that included some of the most promising and original young writers of the time—Mikhail Zoshchenko, Vsevolod Ivanov, Valentin Katayev, Veniamin Kaverin, Konstantin Fedin, Lev Lunts, Nikolay Tikhonov, Victor Shklovsky, and others. Differing in temperament, method, and scope, they were united in their insistence on creative freedom, on the artist's right to pursue his own individual vision, on variety, experimentation in form, and the importance of craft.

Lev Lunts, one of the most brilliant members of the group, formulated a manifesto in which he proclaimed the complete autonomy of art. "Literary chimeras," he wrote, "are a special form of reality." He rejected those on both the right and the left who cried, "If you are not with us, you are against us." "With whom are we, the Serapion Brethren?" he asked. "We are with the hermit Serapion. . . . We reject utilitarianism. We do not write for the sake of propaganda. Art is as real as life itself, and, as life itself, it has no goal or meaning, it exists because it must exist. . . . Our one demand is that the writer's voice must never be false."

The Serapions rallied round Zamyatin's credo that "true literature can exist only where it is created, not by diligent and trustworthy officials, but by madmen, hermits, heretics, dreamers, rebels, and skeptics,"—a credo he proclaimed in 1921, in his essay "I Am Afraid."* And the need for heresy, the right to say "no" to official dogma, the belief that mistakes are more useful than truths, that truths are ideas "already afflicted with arteriosclerosis" are urged again and again in Zamyatin's writings. In "Tomorrow" he wrote:

He who has found his ideal today is like Lot's wife, already turned into a pillar of salt. . . . The world is kept alive only by heretics: the heretic Christ, the heretic Copernicus, the heretic Tolstoy. Our symbol of faith is heresy. . . . We call the Russian intelligentsia to the defense of man, and of human values. We appeal, not to those who reject today in the name of a return to yesterday, not to those who are hopelessly deafened by today; we appeal to those who see the distant tomorrow—and judge today in the name of tomorrow, in the name of man.

---

* This essay, as well as the others quoted here, may be found in *A Soviet Heretic: Essays by Yevgeny Zamyatin* (Chicago University Press, 1970).

In 1921, in an essay entitled "Paradise," Zamyatin again lashed out scathingly at the purveyors of unanimity, at those who pressed for total conformity:

Much has been said by many about the imperfection of the universe . . . its astonishing lack of monism: water and fire, mountains and abysses, saints and sinners. What absolute simplicity, what happiness, unclouded by any thought, there would have been if [God] had from the very first created a single firewater, if he had from the very first spared man the savage state of freedom! . . . We are unquestionably living in a cosmic era—an era of creation of a new heaven and a new earth. And naturally we will not repeat [His] mistake. There shall be no more polyphony or dissonances. There shall be only majestic, monumental, all-encompassing unanimity.

In "The New Russian Prose" (1923) he wrote:

Life itself today has lost its plane reality: it is projected, not along the old fixed points, but along the dynamic coordinates of Einstein, of Revolution. In this new projection, the best-known formulas and objects become displaced, fantastic, familiar-unfamiliar. This is why it is so logical for literature today to be drawn to the fantastic plot, or to an amalgam of reality and fantasy.

And in his essay "On Literature, Revolution, Entropy and Other Matters," he developed further one of the central ideas of *We:*

Revolution is everywhere, in everything. It is infinite. There is no final revolution, no final number. The social revolution is only one of an infinite number of numbers. The law of revolution is not a social law, but an immeasurably greater one. It is a cosmic, universal law—like the laws of the conservation of energy and of the dissipation of energy (entropy). . . .

In the same essay he wrote:

Harmful literature is more useful than useful literature, for it is antientropic, it is a means of combating calcification. . . . It is utopian, absurd. . . . It is right 150 years later.

And, one of his most significant statements:

What we need in literature today are vast philosophic horizons. . . . We need the most ultimate, the most fearsome, the most fearless "Why?" and "What next?"

In 1926, in "The Goal," Zamyatin made a frontal attack on the Communist critics who demanded of the writer total subservience to the demands of the party:

The Revolution does not need dogs who "sit up" in expectation of a handout or because they fear the whip. Nor does it need trainers of such dogs. It needs writers who fear nothing. . . . It needs writers in whom the Revolution awakens a true organic echo. And it does not matter if this echo is individual . . . if a writer ignores such-and-such a paragraph adopted at such-and-such a conference. What matters is that his work be sincere, that it lead the reader forward . . . that it disturb the reader rather than reassure and lull his mind. . . . But where forward? And how far forward? The farther the better. . . . Reduction of prices, better sanitation in the cities . . . all this is very good. . . . I can imagine an excellent newspaper article on these topics (an article that will be forgotten the next day). But I find it difficult to imagine a work by Lev Tolstoy or Romain Rolland based on improvement of sanitation.

Inevitably, Zamyatin became one of the prime victims of the purveyors of "unanimity" and "sanitary" literature. He was attacked for "inconsonance with the revolution," for "vilification and slander" of revolutionary tenets and "achievements," for being "a cold and hostile observer" and an "internal émigré" who played into the hands of the enemies of the Soviet regime. (It is scarcely necessary to point here to the long list of independent artists—Akhmatova, Zoshchenko, Pasternak, Brodsky, Solzhenitsyn and others—who have suffered similar treatment at the hands of the dictatorship.)

During the first post-revolutionary decade it was still possible for Zamyatin to publish his works, despite the constant chorus of abuse from the guardians of orthodoxy. His works, naturally, never appeared in the officially sponsored and subsidized magazines. They were usually published in fairly short-lived journals or anthologies issued by writers' groups, or by the few private journals and publishing houses that were still allowed to exist in those early years.

With great courage and integrity, Zamyatin continued to write as he saw and felt—essays, plays, fiction—although the dead hand of the dictatorship was steadily becoming heavier. A striking light on an important facet of his character is thrown by a passage from an essay "On the Future of the Theater," written considerably later and published in French in 1932. "The most serious play," he wrote, "is the play with fate which carries in its pocket a timetable, drawn up and stamped a long time ago, and marking the day and hour of the tragic end of every one of us." Unquestionably, he knew what was to come, but went on doing what he felt he must do.

The scope and quality of his writing, under the circumstances, are astonishing. Zamyatin was not only a consummate satirist and stylist, but a master of many themes and many styles. Some of his stories* are marvelous evocations of the almost mythical old Russia of his childhood. Some read like ballads—the landscape is stark, the people and events tragic or comic on a grand scale. Still others deal with the present, often drawn in a grotesque, oblique, surrealist light, with echoing images and an extraordinary mingling of reality and irreality, mockery and grief. Others are jests, ribald inventions he called "impious tales." In addition to his other qualities, Zamyatin had an unexpected streak of irrepressible gaiety and a great sense of fun.

The same richness and diversity and a keen eye for the comic and grotesque infuse his plays. Many of his characters are marvelous caricatures. Wit, imagination, and, always, most meticulous craftsmanship are combined in much of his work with a profound sense of history and a prophetic vision. This is particularly true of *We,* a searing satire, among other things, on schematic—hence, necessarily, totalitarian—society, written in 1920–1921. *We* was not admitted to publication. Read, as the custom frequently was in those years, at a meeting of the All-Russian Writers' Union in 1923, it elicited a new wave of violent attacks from party-line critics and writers.

Zamyatin wrote this remarkably prophetic novel when the totalitarian future was just becoming discernible. Like all great satirists, he projected from present trends and intimations to an encompassing vision of the society to come. His method, as he defined it in *We,* was *reductio ad finem*—a method later applied with powerful effect by such master satirists as William Golding (*The Inheritors, Lord of the Flies*) and Anthony Burgess (*The Wanting Seed, A Clockwork Orange*).

---

* See *The Dragon: 15 Stories by Yevgeny Zamyatin* (Chicago University Press, 1976).

Poet, mocker (laughter, he wrote, is the most devastating weapon), heretical fighter for freedom and independence in art and in life, Zamyatin was a consistent enemy of all canonized ideas, all coercion, all the purveyors of "compulsory salvation." He mercilessly attacked and ridiculed the emerging totalitarianism, its fawning mediocrities, its reign of brutality, its violation and destruction of the free and creative human spirit. He foresaw it all: the terror, the betrayals, the dehumanization; the ubiquitous "guardians"; the control of thought and action; the constant brainwashing which resulted either in unquestioning automatons or in hypocrites who lied for the sake of survival; the demand that everybody worship the Benefactor, with his huge hand that literally "liquidates," reduces all who dissent, all who passionately want to be themselves to a puddle of clear water. He also foresaw the subjection of the arts. His hero boasts: "We have harnessed the once wild element of poetry. Today, poetry is no longer the idle, impudent whistling of a nightingale; poetry is civic service, poetry is useful." And not only must the people ("numbers") in this apocalyptic state of ritualized totalitarianism attend the gala ceremony of extermination of every heretic by the Benefactor, but a poet is obliged to recite an ode celebrating the wisdom and great justice of the executioner.

In its style, too, *We* is a remarkable achievement, for Zamyatin had a perfect ear and perfect taste. "The language of our epoch is sharp and rapid as a code," he wrote in 1923. In *We*, which is as carefully structured as a poem, the reader will find none of the slow, singing richness of his provincial stories, none of the sly laughter of his "impious tales." *We*, about the square state and square men, is written in a style of utmost severity and discipline—a style in perfect harmony with the author's intention, with the totally controlled society he evokes, where emotion is banished (yet survives), where every moment is lived according to schedule in a glass-enclosed city of glass houses and absolute straight lines, where even lovemaking is done on scheduled days and scheduled hours.

But just as Zamyatin was much more than a keen political intellect, so *We*, within the astonishing discipline of its style, is much more than a political statement. It is a complex philosophical novel of endless subtlety and nuance, allusion and reflections. It is also a profoundly moving human tragedy, and a study in the variety of human loves (passion—D-503; domination—I-330; jealousy—U; tenderness, and gentle, total giving of the self—O-90). And, though the people are nameless "numbers," they are never schematic figures; each is an individual, convincingly and movingly alive.

Zamyatin's main concern in the novel is the problem of man in its multiple aspects: the relation of the individual to society and to other men; the conflict between the tempting safety of unfreedom and the will to free identity; the fear and the lure of alienation; the rift between the rational and the irrational. *We* is also a study of a society that claims to be based on the purely rational—and hence becomes deadly, dehumanizing, absurd.

"Who are they?" the hero asks after he has seen the gentle, hairy creatures outside the Wall that encloses the One State. "The half we have lost?" The feeling half. The irrational half that lives outside of schedules and straight lines. Yet even in the One State, where nothing spontaneous is permitted, the state that is walled off from everything unstructured and alive, life and humanity assert themselves. The hero—a builder and mathematician who has been thoroughly shaped by his society, who never questions it—has atavistic "hairy hands." Seduced into violent and irrational passion, he makes a shocking discovery of an unsuspected, long-suppressed realm—the realm within, of individual identity, of self. "Who am I? What am I like?" he cries despairingly. In a supremely tragicomic scene, he visits a doctor, seeking help against this terrifying malady. The doctor gravely tells him he is seriously ill—he has developed a soul. "Is it dangerous?" he asks. "Incurable," the doctor replies. But, alas, it turns out to be curable in the end. The Benefactor's men have found a remedy for individuality, for rebellion, for humanity: a simple operation to excise the seat of all infection—imagination—and reduce all citizens of the One State to grinning semi-morons.

We is more multifaceted, less hopeless than Orwell's *1984*, written more than twenty-five years later and directly influenced by Zamyatin's novel. Despite its tragic ending, *We* still carries a note of hope. Despite the rout of the rebellion, "there is still fighting in the western parts of the city." Many "numbers" have escaped beyond the Wall. Those who died were not destroyed as human beings—they died fighting and unsubmissive. And though the hero is reduced to an obedient automaton, certain that "Reason" and static order will prevail, though the woman he loved briefly and was forced into betraying dies (as do the poets and rebels she led), the woman who loves him, who is gentle and tender, is safe beyond the Wall. She will bear his child in freedom. And the Wall itself has been proved vulnerable after all. It has been breached—and surely will be breached again.

In *We*, Zamyatin says: This is where we are going. Stop while there is still time. Throughout the poetry and the mockery, there is great warmth—for Russia, for man—and profound grief over the particularly intense ordeals they were to suffer in our century of terror, so uncannily foreseen in the novel, and so proudly faced. For Zamyatin, himself to such an extreme degree a victim of these ordeals, is remarkable in his utter lack of cynicism or bitterness. Anger, mockery, rebellion—but no self-pity and no bitterness. He seems to be saying to all the dogmatists, all who attempt to force life into a rigid mold: You will not, you cannot prevail. Man will not be destroyed.

Zamyatin called *We* "my most jesting and most serious work." And, though it speaks on many levels and of many things, its political message is unmistakable. It is a warning, and a challenge, and a call to action. It is perhaps the fullest statement of Zamyatin's intellectual philosophy and emotional concerns.

Significantly enough, the hounding of Zamyatin rose to fever pitch in the late 1920s, when the present had become too uncomfortably like the prophecy, when the Benefactor and his Machine had become too recognizable as living, immediate realities. In 1929 full power in the literary field was placed in the hands of the RAPP (the Russian Association of Proletarian Writers) which became the instrument for the extirpation of all that was still independent in Russian literature. By campaigns of vilification, by pressure on journals and publishers, by calls for police methods, it sought to bend everyone to the requisite line—service to the party. The RAPP plunged into the role of executioner with gusto, and the results were quickly apparent. Many journals and publishing houses were closed. There was a wave of suicides among writers and poets. Recantations became epidemic. Endless nonparty writers, their spirits broken, publicly repented of their sins and came into the fold, repudiating and rewriting their own works.

A particularly vicious campaign was launched

against Zamyatin and Pilnyak. The latter was pilloried for the publication abroad of his novel *Mahogany*. *We*, which had been written almost ten years earlier and never published in the Soviet Union, was used as the immediate pretext for Zamyatin's destruction. While its first translation into English (in 1924) and Czech (in 1927) had not provoked any noticeable response by Soviet authorities, its publication in 1927 in *Volya Rossii*, a Russian émigré journal published in Czechoslovakia, without the author's knowledge or consent, was used, two years later, as a convenient excuse for bringing the full weight of official pressure upon its author. The matter was discussed at a meeting of the Writers' Union in the summer of 1929, when Zamyatin was away on a summer journey. One after another, his frightened and subservient colleagues rose to denounce him. Zamyatin replied with an indignant and courageous letter, resigning from the Union. "I find it impossible," he wrote, "to belong to a literary organization which ... takes part in the persecution of a fellow member."

Pilnyak was unable to withstand the pressure and recanted. Zamyatin's former pupils and admirers—Ivanov, Katayev, Kaverin—sacrificed their talents to become hacks, manufacturing whatever was required in the shape and style demanded. Those with stronger backbones, like Isaac Babel, turned silent. And only isolated giants like Zamyatin and Bulgakov refused to submit. Denied access to publication, their plays withdrawn from the stage despite enormous popular success, and their books withdrawn from stores and libraries, they wrote to Stalin requesting permission to leave Russia. Both spoke of the ban on their work as a literary death sentence.

Thanks to Gorky's intercession with Stalin,

Zamyatin's request was, surprisingly, granted. He left Russia in 1931 and settled in Paris. His last years were a time of great loneliness and privation. He died of heart disease in 1937, his funeral attended by a mere handful of friends, for he had not accepted the émigré community as his own. To the end he regarded himself as a Soviet writer, waiting merely, as he had written in his letter to Stalin, until "it becomes possible in our country to serve great ideas without cringing before little men," until "there is at least a partial change in the prevailing view concerning the role of the literary artist." He was never to see that day. His death went unmentioned in the Soviet press. Like the rebellious poet of *We,* and like so many of the greatest Russian poets and writers of the twentieth century, he was literally "liquidated"—reduced to nonbeing. His name was deleted from literary histories, and for decades he has been unknown in his homeland.

And yet, he lives. As his fellow victim Bulgakov said, "manuscripts don't burn." He has been revived in the Western world. *We* has been translated into more than ten languages. Many of his stories, essays, and plays have been published abroad in Russian, and also in English translation. Even in Soviet Russia his name is beginning in recent years to crop up (timidly) in occasional memoirs, in occasional obscure essays on science fiction and utopian literature. It has even been restored to literary encyclopedias—of course, with the inevitable negative comment. And although his writings are still unavailable in Soviet Russia, they have undoubtedly reached some readers, writers, and scholars in underground ways, for his influence is clear in the thinking of dissidents of the sixties and seventies. (Their fate, alas, is still much like Zamyatin's. Some are silent, others forced into exile.)

Like all major works of art, *We* lends itself to a multiplicity of interpretations. Numerous essays and analyses have been written on Zamyatin,* and on *We*, approaching it from various points of view and within various frameworks: as a study of modern man alienated from his natural self; as a Freudian charade; as myth presenting man's dilemma in terms of archetypes and dream figures; as a religious parable with strong Dostoyevskian influences; as one of the most significant modern anti-utopias, and so on. *We* is all these, and more. It is one of the great tragic novels of our time.

But let the book speak for itself. The discerning reader will find in it far more than can be suggested in an introduction.

MIRRA GINSBURG

---

* A fine biographical and critical study by Alex M. Shane appeared in the United States in 1968—*The Life and Works of Evgenij Zamjatin* (Berkeley, 1968) containing among other things, an excellent bibliography.

Acknowledgments

We was first published in Russian in book form in 1952 by the Chekhov Publishing House in New York. I wish to express my gratitude to the National Board of Young Men's Christian Associations, present owner of legal rights to books published by the Chekhov Publishing House, for permission to translate *We* into English.

Thanks are also due to the University of Chicago Press for permission to quote from *A Soviet Heretic: Essays by Yevgeny Zamyatin,* published in 1970.

First Entry

TOPICS: A Proclamation
The Wisest of Lines
A Poem

I shall simply copy, word for word, the proclamation that appeared today in the *One State Gazette:*

The building of the *Integral* will be completed in one hundred and twenty days. The great historic hour when the first *Integral* will soar into cosmic space is drawing near. One thousand years ago your heroic ancestors subdued the entire terrestrial globe to the power of the One State. Yours will be a still more glorious feat: you will integrate the infinite equation of the universe with the aid of the fire-breathing, electric, glass *Integral.* You will subjugate the unknown beings on other planets, who may still be living in the primitive condition of freedom, to the beneficent yoke of reason. If they fail to understand that we bring them mathematically infallible happiness, it will be our duty to compel them to be happy. But before resorting to arms, we shall try the power of words.

In the name of the Benefactor, therefore, we proclaim to all the numbers of the One State:

Everyone who feels capable of doing so must compose tracts, odes, manifestoes, poems, or other works extolling the beauty and the grandeur of the One State.

This will be the first cargo to be carried by the *Integral*.

Long live the One State, long live the numbers, long live the Benefactor!

I write this, and I feel: my cheeks are burning. Yes, to integrate the grandiose cosmic equation. Yes, to unbend the wild, primitive curve and straighten it to a tangent—an asymptote—a straight line. For the line of the One State is the straight line. The great, divine, exact, wise straight line—the wisest of all lines.

I, D-503, Builder of the *Integral*, am only one of the mathematicians of the One State. My pen, accustomed to figures, does not know how to create the music of assonances and rhymes. I shall merely attempt to record what I see and think, or, to be more exact, what we think (precisely so—we, and let this *We* be the title of my record). But since this record will be a derivative of our life, of the mathematically perfect life of the One State, will it not be, of itself, and regardless of my will or skill, a poem? It will. I believe, I know it.

I write this, and my cheeks are burning. This must be similar to what a woman feels when she first senses within herself the pulse of a new, still tiny, still blind little human being. It is I, and at the same time, not I. And for many long months it will be necessary to nourish it with my own life, my own blood, then tear it painfully from myself and lay it at the feet of the One State.

But I am ready, like every one, or almost every one, of us. I am ready.

Second Entry

TOPICS: Ballet
Square Harmony
X

Spring. From beyond the Green Wall, from the wild, invisible plains, the wind brings yellow honey pollen of some unknown flowers. The sweet pollen dries your lips, and every minute you pass your tongue over them. The lips of all the women you see must be sweet (of the men, too, of course). This interferes to some extent with the flow of logical thought.

But the sky! Blue, unblemished by a single cloud. (How wild the tastes of the ancients, whose poets could be inspired by those absurd, disorderly, stupidly tumbling piles of vapor!) I love—I am certain I can safely say, we love—only such a sterile, immaculate sky. On days like this the whole world is cast of the same impregnable, eternal glass as the Green Wall, as all our buildings. On days like this you see the bluest depth of things, their hitherto unknown, astonishing equations—you see them even in the most familiar everyday objects.

Take, for instance, this. In the morning I was at the dock where the *Integral* is being built, and suddenly I *saw:* the lathes; the regulator spheres rotating with closed eyes, utterly oblivious of all; the cranks flashing, swinging left and right; the balance beam proudly swaying its shoulders; the bit of the slotting machine dancing up and down in time to unheard music. Suddenly I saw the whole beauty of this grandiose mechanical ballet, flooded with pale blue sunlight.

And then, to myself: Why is this beautiful? Why is dance beautiful? Answer: because it is *unfree* motion, because the whole profound meaning of dance lies precisely in absolute, esthetic subordination, in ideal unfreedom. And if it is true that our forebears abandoned themselves to dance at the most exalted moments of their lives (religious mysteries, military parades), it means only one thing: the instinct of unfreedom is organically inherent in man from time immemorial, and we, in our present life, are only consciously. . . .

I will have to finish later: the annunciator clicked. I looked up: O-90, of course. In half a minute she'll be here, for our daily walk.

Dear O! It always seems to me that she looks exactly like her name: about ten centimeters shorter than the Maternal Norm, and therefore carved in the round, all of her, with that pink O, her mouth, open to meet every word I say. And also, that round, plump fold on her wrist, like a baby's.

When she came in, the flywheel of logic was still humming at full swing within me, and I began, by sheer force of inertia, to speak to her about the formula I had just established, which encompassed everything—dance, machines, and all of us.

"Marvelous, isn't it?" I asked.

"Yes, marvelous." O-90 smiled rosily at me. "It's spring."

4

Well, wouldn't you know: spring ... She talks about spring. Women ... I fell silent.

Downstairs, the avenue was full. In such weather, the afternoon personal hour is used for an additional walk. As always, the Music Plant played the "March of the One State" with all its trumpets. The numbers walked in even ranks, four abreast, ecstatically stepping in time to the music— hundreds, thousands of numbers, in pale blue unifs,* with golden badges on their breasts, bearing the State Number of each man and woman. And I—the four of us—but one of the innumerable waves in this mighty stream. On my left, O-90 (if this were being written by one of my hairy ancestors a thousand years ago, he probably would have described her by that funny word "mine"); on my right, two numbers I did not know, male and female.

Blessedly blue sky, tiny baby suns in every badge, faces unshadowed by the insanity of thoughts ... Rays. Do you understand that? Everything made of some single, radiant, smiling substance. And the brass rhythms: "Ta-ta-ta-tam! Ta-ta-ta-tam!" Like brass stairs gleaming in the sun, and every step taking you higher and higher, into the dizzying blue. ...

And again, as this morning at the dock, I saw everything as though for the first time in my life: the straight, immutable streets, the glittering glass of the pavements, the divine parallelepipeds of the transparent houses, the square harmony of the gray-blue ranks. And I felt: it was not the generations before me, but I—yes, I—who had conquered the old God and the old life. It was I who had created all this. And I was like a tower, I dared not

---

* Derived apparently from the ancient "uniform."

move an elbow lest walls, cupolas, machines tumble in fragments about me.

Then—a leap across the centuries, from $+$ to $-$. I remembered (evidently an association by contrast) —I suddenly remembered a picture I had seen in a museum: one of their avenues, out of the twentieth century, dazzlingly motley, a teeming crush of people, wheels, animals, posters, trees, colors, birds. . . . And they say this had really existed—could exist. It seemed so incredible, so preposterous that I could not contain myself and burst out laughing.

And immediately, there was an echo—laughter—on my right. I turned: a flash of white—extraordinarily white and sharp teeth, an unfamiliar female face.

"Forgive me," she said, "but you looked at everything around you with such an inspired air, like some mythical god on the seventh day of creation. It seems to me you are sure that even I was created by you, and by no one else. I am very flattered. . . ."

All this—without a smile; I would even say, with a certain deference (perhaps she knew that I am the Builder of the *Integral*). But in the eyes, or in the eyebrows—I could not tell—there was a certain strange, irritating X, which I could not capture, could not define in figures.

For some odd reason, I felt embarrassed and tried, in a rather stumbling manner, to explain my laughter to her logically. It was entirely clear, I said, that this contrast, this impassable abyss between the present and the past . . .

"But why impassable?" (What white teeth!) "A bridge can be thrown across an abyss. Just think: drums, battalions, ranks—all this has also existed in the past; and, consequently . . ."

"But of course!" I cried. (What an astonishing coincidence of ideas: she spoke almost my own words, the words I had written down before our walk.) "You understand, even ideas. And this is because nobody is 'one,' but 'one of.' We are so alike. . . ."

She: "Are you sure?"

I saw her eyebrows raised to her temples at a sharp angle, like the pointed horns of an X, and again I was confused. I glanced right, left, and . . .

On my right—she, slender, sharp, stubbornly pliant, like a whip, I-330 (I could see her number now) ; on my left—O, altogether different, all curves, with that childish fold on her wrist; and at the other end of our row, a male number I did not know—strange, doubly bent somehow, like the letter S. All of us so different . . .

That one on the right, I-330, seemed to have intercepted my flustered glance, and with a sigh she said, "Yes. . . . Alas!"

Actually, this "alas" was entirely appropriate. But again there was that something in her face, or in her voice. . . . And with a sharpness unusual for me, I said, "No reason for 'Alas.' Science progresses, and it is obvious that, if not now, then in fifty or a hundred years . . ."

"Even everyone's noses . . ."

"Yes," I almost shouted, "noses. If there is any ground for envy, no matter what it is . . . If I have a button-nose and another . . ."

"Oh, your nose is 'classical,' as they used to say in olden times. But your hands . . . No, let us see, let us see your hands!"

I detest to have anyone look at my hands: all hairy, shaggy—a stupid atavism. I held out my hand and said, as indifferently as I could, "An ape's hands."

She glanced at my hands, then at my face. "A most interesting conjunction." She weighed me with her eyes as on a scale, and the horns flicked again at the corners of her eyebrows.

"He is registered with me." O-90's lips opened rosily, with eager joy.

I wished she had kept silent—this was altogether out of place. Generally, this dear O . . . how shall I put it . . . her tongue is wrongly timed; the speed of the tongue should always be some seconds behind the speed of thought, but certainly not the other way around.

At the end of the avenue, the bell on the Accumulator Tower was loudly striking seventeen. The personal hour was over. I-330 was leaving with the S-shaped male number. His face somehow inspired respect, and now it seemed familiar. I must have met him somewhere, but where?

In parting, I-330 said with another of her X-smiles, "Come to auditorium 112 the day after tomorrow."

I shrugged. "If I am assigned to that auditorium . . ."

And she, with an odd certainty, "You will be."

The woman affected me as unpleasantly as an irresolvable irrational member that has somehow slipped into an equation. And I was glad to remain for at least a few moments alone with dear O.

Hand in hand, we crossed four lines of avenues. At the corner she had to turn right, and I, left.

"I'd like so much to come to you today and let down the blinds. Today, right now . . ." O timidly raised her round, blue-crystal eyes to me.

How funny she is. What could I say to her? She had come to me only the day before, and she knew as well as I did that our next sexual day was the day after tomorrow. It was simply a case of her usual "words ahead of thought"—like the occasional (and sometimes damaging) premature supply of a spark to a motor.

Before we parted, I kissed her lovely blue eyes, unshadowed by a single cloud, two—no, let me be precise—three times.

I have just looked over what I had written yesterday, and I see that I did not express myself clearly enough. Of course, it is all entirely clear to any of us. But perhaps you, the unknown readers to whom the *Integral* will bring my notes, have reached only that page in the great book of civilization that our ancestors read some nine hundred years ago. Perhaps you do not know even about such elementary things as the Table of Hours, the Personal Hour, the Maternity Norm, the Green Wall, and the Benefactor. It seems to me ridiculous yet very difficult to speak about all this. It is as if a writer of, say, the twentieth century had to explain in his novel the meaning of "coat," or "apartment," or "wife." Yet, if his novel were to be translated for savages, how could he avoid explaining what a "coat" meant?

I am certain that a savage would look at the "coat" and wonder, "What is it for? It's only a hindrance." It seems to me that your response may be exactly the same when I tell you that none of us has been beyond the Green Wall since the Two Hundred Years' War.

But, my dear readers, a man must think, at least a little. It helps. After all, it is clear that the entire history of mankind, insofar as we know it, is the history of transition from nomadic to increasingly settled forms of existence. And does it not follow that the most settled form (ours) is at the same time the most perfect (ours)? People rushed about from one end of the earth to the other only in prehistoric times, when there were nations, wars, commerce, discoveries of all sorts of Americas. But who needs that now? What for?

I admit, the habit of such settled existence was not achieved easily, or all at once. During the Two Hundred Years' War, when all the roads fell into ruin and were overgrown with grass, it must at first have seemed extremely inconvenient to live in cities cut off from one another by green jungles. But what of it? After man's tail dropped off, it must have been quite difficult for him at first to learn to drive off flies without its aid. In the beginning he undoubtedly missed his tail. But now—can you imagine yourself with a tail? Or can you imagine yourself in the street naked, without a coat? (For you may still be trotting about in "coats.") And so it is with me: I cannot imagine a city that is not clad in a Green Wall; I cannot imagine a life that is not regulated by the figures of our Table.

The Table ... At this very moment, from the wall in my room, its purple figures on a field of gold stare tenderly and sternly into my eyes. Involuntarily, my mind turns to what the ancients called an "icon," and I long to compose poems or prayers (which are the same thing). Oh, why am I not a poet, to render fitting praise to the Table, the heart and pulse of the One State!

As schoolchildren we all read (perhaps you

have, too) that greatest literary monument to have come down to us from ancient days—"The Railway Guide." But set it side by side with our Table, and it will be as graphite next to a diamond: both consist of the same element—carbon—yet how eternal, how transparent is the diamond, how it gleams! Whose breath will fail to quicken as he rushes clattering along the pages of "The Railway Guide"? But our Table of Hours! Why, it transforms each one of us into a figure of steel, a six-wheeled hero of a mighty epic poem. Every morning, with six-wheeled precision, at the same hour and the same moment, we—millions of us—get up as one. At the same hour, in million-headed unison, we start work; and in million-headed unison we end it. And, fused into a single million-handed body, at the same second, designated by the Table, we lift our spoons to our mouths. At the same second, we come out for our walk, go to the auditorium, go to the hall for Taylor exercises, fall asleep. . . .

I shall be entirely frank: even we have not yet found an absolute, precise solution to the problem of happiness. Twice a day, from sixteen to seventeen, and from twenty-one to twenty-two, the single mighty organism breaks up into separate cells; these are the Personal Hours designated by the Table. In these hours you will see modestly lowered shades in the rooms of some; others will walk with measured tread along the avenue, as though climbing the brass stairs of the March; still others, like myself now, are at their desks. But I am confident—and you may call me an idealist and dreamer—I am confident that sooner or later we shall fit these Personal Hours as well into the general formula. Some day these 86,400 seconds will also be entered in the Table of Hours.

I have read and heard many incredible things

about those times when people still lived in a free, i.e., unorganized, savage condition. But most incredible of all, it seems to me, is that the state authority of that time—no matter how rudimentary —could allow men to live without anything like our Table, without obligatory walks, without exact regulation of mealtimes, getting up and going to bed whenever they felt like it. Some historians even say that in those times the street lights burned all night, and people walked and drove around in the streets at all hours of the night.

Try as I may, I cannot understand it. After all, no matter how limited their intelligence, they should have understood that such a way of life was truly mass murder—even if slow murder. The state (humaneness) forbade the killing of a single individual, but not the partial killing of millions day by day. To kill one individual, that is, to diminish the total sum of human lives by fifty years, was criminal. But to diminish the sum of human lives by fifty million years was not considered criminal. Isn't that absurd? Today, any ten-year-old will solve this mathematical-moral problem in half a minute. They, with all their Kants taken together, could not solve it (because it never occurred to any of the Kants to build a system of scientific ethics, i.e., ethics based on subtraction, addition, division, and multiplication).

And wasn't it absurd that the state (it dared to call itself a state!) could leave sexual life without any semblance of control? As often and as much as anyone might wish. . . . Totally unscientific, like animals. And blindly, like animals, they bore their young. Isn't it ridiculous: to know agriculture, poultry-breeding, fish-breeding (we have exact information that they knew all this), yet fail to go on to the ultimate step of this logical ladder—

13

child-breeding; fail to establish such a thing as our Maternal and Paternal Norms.

It is so absurd, so unbelievable, that I am afraid, as I write this, that you, my unknown readers, will think me a malicious joker. I am afraid you may decide that I am merely trying to mock you, telling you utter nonsense with a straight face.

But, to begin with, I am incapable of jokes, for every joke contains a lie as an implicit function. Secondly, our One State Science asserts that this was how the ancients lived, and our State Science never errs. Besides, where would state logic have come from at a time when men were living in the condition of freedom—the condition of animals, apes, the herd? What could be expected of them, when even in our time the wild, apelike echo still occasionally rises from somewhere below, from some shaggy depth?

Fortunately, only on rare occasions. Fortunately, they are only breakdowns of minor parts which can easily be repaired without halting the eternal, grandiose movement of the entire Machine. And to expel the warped bolt, we have the skilled, heavy hand of the Benefactor and the experienced eyes of the Guardians.

And, by the way, I've just remembered. That number I saw yesterday, bent like an S—I think I've seen him coming out of the Office of the Guardians. Now I understand that instinctive feeling of respect I had for him, and the sense of awkwardness when the strange I-330 spoke before him. . . . I must confess that this I-330 . . .

The bell for bedtime: it is past twenty-two. Until tomorrow.

Fourth Entry

Until now, everything in life was clear to me (no wonder I seem to have a predilection for the very word "clear"). Yet today ... I cannot understand it.

First: I was, indeed, assigned to auditorium 112, as she had told me. Although the probability was $\dfrac{1500}{10,000,000} = \dfrac{3}{20,000}$ (1500 being the number of auditoriums; 10,000,000, the number of numbers). And, second ... But let me tell it in order, as it happened.

The auditorium—an enormous, sun-drenched hemisphere of massive glass. Circular rows of nobly spherical, smooth-shaven heads. With a slightly palpitating heart I looked around me. I think I was searching for the sight of a rosy crescent—O's sweet lips—over the blue waves of unifs. A flash of someone's extraordinarily white, sharp teeth, like ... No, but it wasn't that. O was to come to me at

15

twenty-one that evening. It was entirely natural for me to wish to see her there.

The bell rang. We stood up and sang the Hymn of the One State. And then, from the stage, the voice of the phono-lecturer, glittering with its golden loud-speakers and wit.

"Respected numbers! Our archeologists have recently dug up a certain twentieth-century book in which the ironic author tells the story of a savage and a barometer. The savage noticed that every time the barometer indicated 'rain,' it actually rained. And since he wanted it to rain, he picked out exactly enough mercury from the column to leave it at 'rain.'" (On the screen—a savage, dressed in feathers, picking out the mercury. Laughter.) "You are laughing. But does it not seem to you that the European of that period was even more ridiculous? Like the savage, the European wanted 'rain'—rain with a capital letter, algebraic rain. But all he did was stand before the barometer like a limp wet hen. The savage, at least, had more courage and energy and logic, if only primitive logic. He had been able to discover that there was a connection between effect and cause. Picking out the mercury, he was able to take the first step on that great road along which . . ."

At this point (I repeat, I write these notes without concealing anything)—at this point I became as though impermeable to the vitalizing stream that flowed from the loud-speakers. I was suddenly overcome by the feeling that I had come there for nothing (why "for nothing," and how could I not have come, since I had been assigned there?). Everything seemed empty to me, nothing but mere husks. And when, by dint of a considerable effort, I managed to switch on my attention again, the phono-lecturer had already gone on to his main topic: our music, mathematical composition. (The mathematician as the cause, music as the effect.) He was describing the recently devised musicometer.

"Simply by turning this handle, any of you can produce up to three sonatas an hour. Yet think how much effort this had cost your forebears! They were able to create only by whipping themselves up to fits of 'inspiration'—an unknown form of epilepsy. And here you have a most amusing illustration of what they produced: Scriabin, the twentieth century. They called this black box" (a curtain parted on the stage, revealing their most ancient instrument) "a 'grand,' a 'royal' instrument, which only shows once more to what extent their entire music . . ."

And then I lost the thread again, perhaps because . . . Yes, I will be frank, because she, I-330, came out to the "royal" box. I suppose I was simply startled by her sudden appearance on the stage.

She wore the fantastic costume of the ancient epoch: a closely fitting black dress, which sharply emphasized the whiteness of her bare shoulders and breast, with that warm shadow, stirring with her breath, between . . . and the dazzling, almost angry teeth. . . .

A smile—a bite—to us, below. Then she sat down and began to play. Something savage, spasmodic, variegated, like their whole life at that time—not a trace of rational mechanical method. And, of course, all those around me were right, they all laughed. Except for a few . . . but why was it that I, too . . . I?

Yes, epilepsy, a sickness of the spirit, pain . . . Slow, sweet pain—a bite—and you want it still deeper, still more painful. Then, slowly, the sun. Not ours, not that bluish, crystal, even glow through glass bricks, no—a wild, rushing, scorching

17

sun—and off with all your clothing, tear everything to shreds.

The number next to me glanced to the left, at me, and snorted. Somehow, a vivid memory remains: a tiny bubble of saliva blew out on his lips and burst. The bubble sobered me. I was myself again.

Like all the others, I now heard only senseless, hurried clattering. I laughed. There was a feeling of relief; everything was simple. The clever phonolecturer had given us too vivid a picture of that primitive age. That was all.

With what enjoyment I listened afterward to our present music! (It was demonstrated at the end, for contrast.) The crystalline chromatic measures of converging and diverging infinite series and the synthesizing chords of Taylor and McLauren formulas; the full-toned, square, heavy tempos of "Pythagoras' Trousers"; the sad melodies of attenuating vibrations; vivid beats alternating with Frauenhofer lines of pauses—like the spectroscopic analysis of planets. . . . What grandeur! What imperishable logic! And how pathetic the capricious music of the ancients, governed by nothing but wild fantasies. . . .

As usual, we walked out through the wide doors of the auditorium in orderly ranks, four abreast. The familiar, doubly bent figure flashed past; I bowed respectfully.

O was to come in an hour. I felt pleasantly and beneficially excited. At home I stepped hurriedly into the office, handed in my pink coupon, and received the certificate permitting me to lower the shades. This right is granted only on sexual days. At all other times we live behind our transparent walls that seem woven of gleaming air—we are always visible, always washed in light. We have nothing to conceal from one another. Besides, this makes much easier the difficult and noble task of the Guardians. For who knows what might happen otherwise? Perhaps it was precisely those strange, opaque dwellings of the ancients that gave rise to their paltry cage psychology. "My (*sic!*) home is my castle." What an idea!

At twenty-two I lowered the shades, and at the same moment O entered, slightly out of breath. She held up to me her pink lips and her pink coupon. I tore off the stub—and could not tear myself away from her pink mouth until the very last second—twenty-two-fifteen.

Afterward I showed her my "notes" and spoke (I think I spoke very well) about the beauty of the square, the cube, the straight line. She listened with such enchanting pink attention, and suddenly a tear dropped from the blue eyes, then a second, a third, right on the open page (page 7). The ink ran. Now I shall have to copy the page.

"Darling D, if only you—if . . ."

"If" what? If . . . Her old song again about a child? Or, perhaps, something new—about . . . about the other one? But this would . . . No, really, it would be too absurd.

Fifth Entry

Again it's all wrong. Again I speak to you, my unknown reader, as though you ... As though, let us say, you were my old friend R-13, the poet, the one with the Negroid lips—everybody knows him. But you are—on the moon, on Venus, Mars, Mercury? Who knows where you are, or who you are.

Now, think of a square, a living, beautiful square. And imagine that it must tell you about itself, about its life. You understand, a square would scarcely ever think of telling you that all its four angles are equal: this has become so natural, so ordinary to it that it's simply no longer consciously aware of it. And so with me: I find myself continually in this square's position. Take the pink coupons, for example, and all the rest that goes with them. To me, this is as natural as the equality of its four angles is to the square, but to you it may be more of a mystery than Newton's binomial theorem.

Well. One of the ancient sages said a clever thing—accidentally, of course—"Love and Hunger rule the world." Ergo: to conquer the world, man must conquer its rulers. Our forebears succeeded, at heavy cost, in conquering Hunger; I am speaking of the Great Two Hundred Years' War—the war between the city and the village. The primitive peasants, prompted perhaps by religious prejudice, stubbornly clung to their "bread." * But in the year 35 before the founding of the One State, our present food, a petroleum product, was developed. True, only 0.2 of the earth's population survived the war. But, cleansed of its millennial filth, how radiant the face of the earth has become! And those two tenths survived to taste the heights of bliss in the shining palace of the One State.

Is it not clear, however, that bliss and envy are the numerator and denominator of the fraction called happiness? And what sense would there be in the countless sacrifices of the Two Hundred Years' War, if reasons for envy still remained in our life? Yet they did remain, for there were still "button" noses and "classical" ones (our conversation during the walk); there were still some whose love was sought by many, and those whose love was sought by none.

Naturally, having conquered Hunger (algebraically, by the sum total of external welfare), the One State launched its attack against the other ruler of the world—Love. And finally this elemental force was also subjugated, i.e., organized and reduced to mathematical order. About three hundred years ago, our historic *Lex Sexualis* was proclaimed: "Each number has a right to any other number, as to a sexual commodity."

Since then it has been only a matter of technolo-

---

* This word has survived only as a poetic metaphor; the chemical composition of this substance is unknown to us.

gy. You are carefully examined in the laboratories of the Sexual Department; the exact content of sexual hormones in your blood is determined, and you are provided with an appropriate Table of sexual days. After that, you declare that on your sexual days you wish to use number so-and-so, and you receive your book of coupons (pink). And that is all.

Clearly, this leaves no possible reasons for envy; the denominator of the happiness fraction is reduced to zero, and the fraction is transformed into a magnificent infinity. And so what to the ancients was the source of innumerable stupid tragedies has been reduced to a harmonious, pleasant, and useful function of the organism, a function like sleep, physical labor, the consumption of food, defecation, and so on. Hence you see how the great power of logic purifies everything it touches. Oh, if only you, my dear readers, would come to know this divine power, if you, too, would learn to follow it to the end!

How strange . . . I have written today about the loftiest peaks of human history; I have breathed all this time the purest mountain air of thought. Yet within me everything is somehow cloudly, cobwebby, shadowed by the cross of a strange, fourpawed X. Or is it my own shaggy paws? And all because they have been so long before my eyes? I dislike to talk about them, and I dislike them: they are a relic of a savage epoch. Can it be that somewhere within me there is really . . .

I wanted to cross out all this, because it is outside the outlined topics for this entry. Then I decided I would leave it. Let my notes, like the most sensitive seismograph, record the curve of even the most insignificant vibrations of my brain: for it is precisely such vibrations that are sometimes the forewarning of . . .

But this is entirely absurd. This really should be stricken out: we have channeled all elemental forces —there can be no catastrophes.

And now all is entirely clear to me. The odd feeling within me is simply the result of that same square position I have described before. And the troubling X is not within me (it cannot be); it is simply my fear that some X may remain in you, my unknown readers. But I am confident you will not judge me too severely. I am confident you will understand that it is far more difficult for me to write than it has been for any other author in the history of mankind. Some wrote for their contemporaries; others for their descendants. But no one has ever written for ancestors, or for beings similar to his primitive, remote ancestors.

Sixth Entry

I repeat: I have made it my duty to write without concealing anything. Therefore, sad as it is, I must note here that even among us the process of the hardening, the crystallization of life has evidently not yet been completed; there are still some steps to be ascended before we reach the ideal. The ideal (clearly) is the condition where nothing *happens* any more. But now . . . Well, today's *One State Gazette* announces that the day after tomorrow there will be a celebration of Justice at the Plaza of the Cube. This means that once again some number has disturbed the operation of the great State Machine; again something has happened that was unforeseen, unforecalculated.

Besides, something has happened to me as well. True, this was during the Personal Hour, that is, at a time especially set aside for unforeseen circumstances. Nevertheless . . .

At about the hour of sixteen (or, to be exact, ten to sixteen) I was at home. Suddenly the telephone rang. A female voice: "D-503?"

24

"Yes."

"Are you free?"

"Yes."

"This is I, I-330. I shall call for you in a moment —we'll go to the Ancient House. Agreed?"

I-330 . . . She irritates and repels me, she almost frightens me. But this is exactly why I said, "Yes."

Five minutes later we were already in the aero. The blue majolica of the Maytime sky; the light sun in its own golden aero buzzing after us, neither falling behind nor overtaking us. And ahead of us—a cloud, white as a cataract, preposterous and puffed out like the cheeks of an ancient cupid, and somehow disturbing. Our front window is up. Wind, drying the lips. Involuntarily, you lick them all the time, and all the time you think of lips.

Then, in the distance, blurred green spots—out there, behind the Wall. A slight, quick sinking of the heart—down, down, down—as from a steep mountain, and we are at the Ancient House.

The whole strange, fragile, blind structure is completely enclosed in a glass shell. Otherwise, of course, it would have fallen apart a long time ago. At the glass door, an old woman, all wrinkled, especially her mouth—nothing but folds and pleats, the lips sunk inward, as if the mouth had grown together somehow. It seemed incredible that she would still be able to speak. And yet, she spoke.

"Well, darlings, so you've come to see my little house?" And the wrinkles beamed (they must have arranged themselves radially, creating the impression of "beaming").

"Yes, Grandmother, I felt like seeing it again," said I-330.

The wrinkles beamed. "What sunshine, eh? Well, well, now? You little pixy! I kno-w, I know! All right, go in by yourselves, I'll stay here, in the sun . . ."

Hm ... My companion must be a frequent guest here. I had a strong desire to shake something off, something annoying: probably the same persistent visual image—the cloud on the smooth blue majolica.

As we ascended the broad, dark staircase, I-330 said, "I love her, that old woman."

"Why?"

"I don't know. Perhaps for her mouth. Or perhaps for no reason. Just like that."

I shrugged. She went on, smiling faintly, or perhaps not smiling at all, "I feel terribly guilty. Obviously, there should be no 'love just like that,' but only 'love because.' All elemental phenomena should . . ."

"It's clear . . ." I began, but immediately caught myself at the word and cast a stealthy glance at I-330: had she noticed it or not?

She was looking down somewhere; her eyes were lowered, like shades.

I thought of the evening hour, at about twenty-two. You walk along the avenue and there, among the bright, transparent cells—the dark ones, with lowered shades. And behind the shades . . . What was behind the shades within her? Why had she called me today, and what was all this for?

I opened a heavy, creaking, opaque door, and we stepped into a gloomy, disorderly place (they called it an "apartment"). The same strange "royal" musical instrument—and again the wild, disorganized, mad music, like the other time—a jumble of colors and forms. A white flat area above; dark blue walls; red, green, and orange bindings of ancient books; yellow bronze—chandeliers, a statue of Buddha; furniture built along lines convulsed in epilepsy, incapable of being fitted into an equation.

I could barely endure all that chaos. But my companion evidently had a stronger organism.

"This is my favorite ..." and suddenly she seemed to catch herself. A bite-smile, white sharp teeth. "I mean, to be exact, the most absurd of all their 'apartments.' "

"Or, to be even more exact," I corrected her, "their states. Thousands of microscopic, eternally warring states, as ruthless as ..."

"Of course, that's clear ..." she said, apparently with utmost seriousness.

We crossed a room with small children's beds (the children at that time were also private property). Then more rooms, glimmering mirrors, somber wardrobes, intolerably gaudy sofas, a huge "fireplace," a large mahogany bed. Our modern—beautiful, transparent, eternal—glass was there only in the pathetic, fragile little window squares.

"And then, imagine! Here they all loved 'just like that,' burning, suffering. ..." (Again the dropped shades of the eyes.) "What stupid, reckless waste of human energy—don't you think?"

She seemed to speak somehow out of myself; she spoke my thoughts. But in her smile there was that constant, irritating X. Behind the shades, something was going on within her—I don't know what—that made me lose my patience. I wanted to argue with her, to shout at her (yes, shout), but I had to agree—it was not possible to disagree.

She stopped before a mirror. At that moment I saw only her eyes. I thought: A human being is made as absurdly as these preposterous "apartments"; human heads are opaque, with only tiny windows in them—the eyes. As though guessing, she turned. "Well, here are my eyes. Well?" (Silently, of course.)

Before me, two eerily dark windows, and within, such a mysterious, alien life. I saw only flame—some fireplace of her own was blazing there—and shapes resembling ...

27

This, of course was natural: I saw myself reflected in her eyes. But what I was feeling was unnatural and unlike me (it must have been the opressive effect of the surroundings). I felt definitely frightened. I felt trapped, imprisoned in that primitive cage, caught by the savage whirlwind of the ancient life.

"You know what," said I-330. "Step out for a moment to the next room." Her voice came from there, from within, from behind the dark windows of her eyes, where the fireplace was blazing.

I went out and sat down. From a shelf on the wall, the snubnosed, asymmetrical physiognomy of some ancient poet (Pushkin, I think) smiled faintly right into my face. Why was I sitting there, meekly enduring that smile? Why all of this? Why was I there—why these ridiculous feelings? That irritating, repellent woman, her strange game . . .

A closet door was shut behind the wall, the rustle of silk. I barely restrained myself from going in and . . . I don't remember exactly—I must have wanted to say very sharp words to her.

But she had already come out. She wore a short, old, vivid yellow dress, a black hat, black stockings. The dress was of light silk. I could see the stockings, very long, much higher than the knees. And the bare throat, and the shadow between . . .

"Look, you are clearly trying to be original, but don't you . . ."

"Clearly," she interrupted me, "to be original is to be in some way distinct from others. Hence, to be original is to violate equality. And that which in the language of the ancients was called 'being banal' is with us merely the fulfillment of our duty. Because . . ."

"Yes, yes! Precisely." I could not restrain myself. "And there is no reason for you to . . . to . . ."

She went over to the statue of the snub-nosed poet and, drawing down the blinds over the wild flame of her eyes, blazing within her, behind her windows, she said a very sensible thing (this time, it seems to me, entirely in earnest, perhaps to mollify me). "Don't you find it astonishing that once upon a time people tolerated such characters? And not only tolerated, but worshiped them? What a slavish spirit! Don't you think?"

"It's clear ... I mean ..." (That damned "It's clear" again!)

"Oh, yes, I understand. But actually, these poets were masters far more powerful than their crowned kings. Why weren't they isolated, exterminated? With us ..."

"Yes, with us ..." I began, and suddenly she burst out laughing. I could see that laughter with my eyes: the resonant sharp curve of it, as pliantly resistant as a whip.

I remember, I trembled all over. Just to seize her, and ... I cannot recall what I wanted to do. But I had to do something, anything. Mechanically I opened my golden badge, glanced at the watch. Ten to seventeen.

"Don't you think it's time?" I said as politely as I could.

"And if I asked you to remain here with me?"

"Look, do you ... do you know what you are saying? In ten minutes I must be in the auditorium. ..."

" ... and all numbers must attend the prescribed courses in art and sciences," she said in my voice. Then she raised the blinds, looked up; the fireplace blazed through the dark windows. "I know a doctor at the Medical Office, he is registered with me. If I ask him, he will give you a certificate that you were sick. Well?"

Now I understood. At last, I understood where that whole game of hers was leading.

"So that's it! And do you know that, like any honest number, I must, in fact, immediately go to the Office of the Guardians and . . ."

"And not 'in fact'?"—sharp smile-bite. "I am terribly curious—will you go to the Office, or won't you?"

"Are you staying?" I put my hand on the doorknob. It was brass, and I heard my voice—it was also brass.

"One moment. . . . May I?"

She went to the telephone, asked for some number—I was too upset to remember it—and cried out, "I shall wait for you in the Ancient House. Yes, yes, alone. . . ."

I turned the cold brass knob.

"You will permit me to take the aero?"

"Yes, certainly! Of course. . . ."

Outside, in the sunshine, at the entrance, the old woman was dozing like a vegetable. Again it was astonishing that her closegrown mouth opened and she spoke.

"And your . . . did she remain there by herself?"

"By herself."

The old woman's mouth grew together again. She shook her head. Evidently, even her failing brain understood the full absurdity and danger of the woman's conduct.

Exactly at seventeen I was at the lecture. And it was only here that I suddenly realized I had said an untruth to the old woman: I-330 was not there by herself now. Perhaps it was this—that I had unwittingly lied to the old woman—that tormented me and interfered with my listening. Yes, she was not by herself: that was the trouble.

After half past twenty-one I had a free hour. I

could go to the Office of the Guardians right there and then and turn in my report. But I felt extremely tired after that stupid incident. And then— the legal time limit for reporting was two days. I would do it tomorrow; I still had twenty-four hours.

TOPICS: An Eyelash
Taylor
Henbane and Lilies of the Valley

Night. Green, orange, blue. Red royal instrument.
Orange-yellow dress. The bronze Buddha. Suddenly he raises his heavy bronze eyelids, and sap begins to flow from them, from Buddha. And sap
from the yellow dress, and drops of sap trickling
down the mirror, and from the large bed, and the
children's beds, and now I myself, flowing with sap
—and some strange, sweet, mortal terror. . . .

I woke: soft, bluish light, glimmer of glass walls,
glass chairs and table. This calmed me; my heart
stopped hammering. Sap, Buddha . . . what nonsense! Clearly I must be ill. I have never dreamed
before. They say that with the ancients dreaming
was a perfectly ordinary, normal occurrence. But of
course, their whole life was a dreadful whirling
carousel—green, orange, Buddhas, sap. We, however, know that dreams are a serious psychic disease.
And I know that until this moment my brain has
been a chronometrically exact gleaming mechanism without a single speck of dust. But now . . .
Yes, precisely: I feel some alien body in my brain,

like the finest eyelash in the eye. You do not feel your body, but that eye with the lash in it—you can't forget it for a second. . . .

The brisk crystal bell over my head: seven o'clock, time to get up. On the right and the left, through the glass walls, I see myself, my room, my clothes, my movements—repeated a thousand times over. This is bracing: you feel yourself a part of a great, powerful, single entity. And the precise beauty of it—not a single superfluous gesture, curve, or turn.

Yes, this Taylor was unquestionably the greatest genius of the ancients. True, his thought did not reach far enough to extend his method to all of life, to every step, to the twenty-four hours of every day. He was unable to integrate his system from one hour to twenty-four. Still, how could they write whole libraries of books about some Kant, yet scarcely notice Taylor, that prophet who was able to see ten centuries ahead?

Breakfast is over. The Hymn of the One State is sung in unison. In perfect rhythm, by fours, we walk to the elevators. The faint hum of motors, and quickly—down, down, down, with a slight sinking of the heart . . .

Then suddenly again that stupid dream—or some implicit function of the dream. Oh, yes, the other day—the descent in the aero. However, all that is over. Period. And it is good that I was so decisive and sharp with her.

In the car of the underground I sped to the place where the graceful body of the *Integral*, still motionless, not yet animated by fire, gleamed in the sun. Shutting my eyes, I dreamed in formulas. Once more I calculated in my mind the initial velocity needed to tear the *Integral* away from the earth. Each fraction of a second the mass of the *Integral* would change (expenditure of the explosive fuel). The equation was very complex, with transcendental values.

As through a dream—in that firm world of numbers—someone sat down next to me, jostled me slightly, said, "Sorry."

I opened my eyes a little. At first glance (association with the *Integral*), something rushing into space: a head—rushing because at either side of it stood out pink wing-ears. Then the curve at the heavy back of the head, the stooped shoulders—double-curved—the letter S . . .

And through the glass walls of my algebraic world, again that eyelash—something unpleasant that I must do today.

"Oh, no, it's nothing. Certainly." I smiled at my neighbor, bowing to him. The number S-4711 glinted from his badge. So this was why I had associated him from the very first with the letter S: a visual impression, unrecorded by the conscious mind. His eyes glinted—two sharp little drills, revolving rapidly, boring deeper and deeper—in a moment they would reach the very bottom and see what I would not . . . even to myself . . .

That troubling eyelash suddenly became entirely clear to me. He was one of them, one of the Guardians, and it was simplest to tell him everything at once, without delay.

"You know, I was at the Ancient House yesterday . . ." My voice was strange, somehow flattened out. I tried to clear my throat.

"Why, that's excellent. It gives material for very instructive conclusions."

"But, you see, I was not alone, I accompanied number I-330, and . . ."

"I-330? I am delighted for you. A very interesting, talented woman. She has many admirers."

But then, perhaps, he too? That time during the walk . . . And he might even be registered for her?

No, it was impossible, unthinkable to talk to him about it; that was clear.

"Oh, yes, yes! Of course, of course! Very." I smiled more and more broadly and foolishly, and I felt: This smile makes me look naked, stupid.

The little gimlets had reached the very bottom, then, whirling rapidly, slipped back into his eyes. With a double-edged smile, S nodded to me and slid away toward the exit.

I hid behind my newspaper—it seemed to me that everyone was staring at me—and instantly forgot about the eyelash, the gimlets, everything. The news I read was so upsetting that it drove all else out of my mind. There was but one short line: "According to reliable sources, new traces have been discovered of the elusive organization which aims at liberation from the beneficent yoke of the State."

"Liberation?" Amazing, the extent to which criminal instincts persist in human nature. I use the word "criminal" deliberately. Freedom and crime are linked as indivisibly as ... well, as the motion of the aero and its speed: when its speed equals zero, it does not move; when man's freedom equals zero, he commits no crimes. That is clear. The only means of ridding man of crime is ridding him of freedom. And now, just as we have gotten rid of it (on the cosmic scale, centuries are, of course, no more than "just"), some wretched half-wits ...

No, I cannot understand why I did not go to the Office of the Guardians yesterday, immediately. Today, after sixteen o'clock, I shall go without fail.

At sixteen-ten I came out, and immediately saw O on the corner—all pink with pleasure at the meeting. "She, now, has a simple, round brain.

35

How fortunate: she will understand and support me. . . ." But no, I needed no support, I had made a firm decision.

The March rang out harmoniously from the trumpets of the Music Plant—the same daily March. What ineffable delight in this daily repetition, its constancy, its mirror clarity!

She seized my hand. "Let's walk." The round blue eyes wide open to me—blue windows—and I could step inside without stumbling against anything; nothing there—that is, nothing extraneous, unnecessary.

"No, no walk today. I must . . ." I told her where I had to go. To my astonishment, the rosy circle of her lips compressed itself into a crescent, its horns down, as if she had tasted something sour. I exploded.

"You female numbers seem to be incurably riddled with prejudices. You are totally incapable of thinking abstractly. You will pardon me, but it is plain stupidity."

"You are going to the spies. . . . Ugh! And I have brought you a spray of lilies of the valley from the Botanical Museum. . . ."

"Why this 'and I'—why the 'and'? Just like a woman." Angrily (I confess) I snatched her lilies of the valley. "All right, here they are, your lilies of the valley! Well? Smell them—it is pleasant, yes? Then why can't you follow just this much logic? Lilies of the valley smell good. Very well. But you cannot speak of smell itself, of the concept 'smell' as either good or bad. You cannot, can you? There is the fragrance of lilies of the valley—and there is the vile stench of henbane: both are smells. There were spies in the ancient state—and there are spies in ours . . . yes, spies. I am not afraid of words. But

36

it is clear that those spies were henbane, and ours are lilies of the valley. Yes, lilies of the valley!"

The pink crescent trembled. I realize now that it only seemed to me—but at that moment I was sure she would burst out laughing. And I shouted still more loudly, "Yes, lilies of the valley. And there is nothing funny about it, nothing at all."

The smooth round spheres of heads floated by and turned to look. O took me gently by the arm. "You are so strange today. . . . You are not ill?"

The dream—yellow—Buddha . . . It instantly became clear to me that I must go to the Medical Office.

"You are right, I'm ill," I cried happily (an incomprehensible contradiction—there was nothing to be happy about).

"Then you must see a doctor at once. You understand yourself—it is your duty to be well. It would be ridiculous for me to try to prove it to you."

"My dear O, of course you are right. Absolutely right!"

I did not go to the Office of the Guardians. It could not be helped, I had to go to the Medical Office; they kept me there until seventeen.

And in the evening (it was all the same now—in the evening the Office of the Guardians was closed) O came to me. The shades were not lowered. We were solving problems from an ancient mathematics textbook: it is very calming and helps to clear the mind. O-90 sat over the exercise book, her head bent to her left shoulder, her tongue diligently pushing out her left cheek. This was so childlike, so enchanting. And within me everything was pleasant, clear, and simple.

She left. I was alone. I took two deep breaths—this is very beneficial before bedtime. Then suddenly, an unscheduled smell, and again something disturbing ... Soon I found it: a spray of lilies of the valley tucked into my bed. Immediately, everything swirled up, rose from the bottom. No, she was simply tactless to leave it there. Very well, I did not go! But it was not my fault that I was sick.

TOPICS: Irrational Root
Triangle
R-13

How long ago it was—during my school years—when I first encountered $\sqrt{-1}$. A vivid memory, as though cut out of time: the brightly lit spherical hall, hundreds of round boys' heads, and Plapa, our mathematics teacher. We nicknamed him Plapa. He was badly worn out, coming apart, and when the monitor plugged him in, the loud-speakers would always start with "Pla-pla-pla-tsh-sh sh," and only then go on to the day's lesson. One day Plapa told us about irrational numbers, and, I remember, I cried, banged my fists on the table, and screamed, "I don't want $\sqrt{-1}$! Take $\sqrt{-1}$ out of me!" This irrational number had grown into me like something foreign, alien, terrifying. It devoured me—it was impossible to conceive, to render harmless, because it was outside *ratio*.

And now again $\sqrt{-1}$. I've just glanced through my notes, and it is clear to me: I have been dodging, lying to myself—merely to avoid seeing the $\sqrt{-1}$. It's nonsense that I was sick, and all the rest of it. I could have gone there. A week ago, I am sure, I would have gone without a moment's hesitation. But now? Why?

Today, too. Exactly at sixteen-ten I stood before the sparkling glass wall. Above me, the golden, sunny, pure gleam of the letters on the sign over the Office. Inside, through the glass, I saw the long line of bluish unifs. Faces glowing like icon lamps in an ancient church: they had come to perform a great deed, to surrender upon the altar of the One State their loved ones, their friends, themselves. And I—I longed to join them, to be with them. And could not: my feet were welded deep into the glass slabs of the pavement, and I stood staring dully, incapable of moving from the spot.

"Ah, our mathematician! Dreaming?"

I started. Black eyes, lacquered with laughter; thick, Negroid lips. The poet R-13, my old friend—and with him, pink O.

I turned angrily. If they had not intruded, I think I finally would have torn the $\sqrt{-1}$ out of myself with the flesh, and entered the Office.

"Not dreaming. Admiring, if you wish!" I answered sharply.

"Certainly, certainly! By rights, my good friend, you should not be a mathematician; you ought to be a poet! Yes! Really, why not transfer to us poets, eh? How would you like that? I can arrange it in a moment, eh?"

R-13 speaks in a rush of words; they spurt out in a torrent and spray comes flying from his thick lips. Every "p" is a fountain; "poets"—a fountain.

"I have served and will continue to serve knowledge," I frowned. I neither like nor understand jokes, and R-13 has the bad habit of joking.

"Oh, knowledge! This knowledge of yours is only cowardice. Don't argue, it's true. You're simply trying to enclose infinity behind a wall, and

40

you are terrified to glance outside the wall. Yes!
Just try and take a look, and you will shut your
eyes. Yes!"

"Walls are the foundation of all human ..." I
began.

R spurted at me like a fountain. O laughed
roundly, rosily. I waved them off—laugh if you
please, it doesn't matter to me. I had other things
to think about. I had to do something to expunge,
to drown out that damned $\sqrt{-1}$.

"Why not come up to my room," I suggested.
"We can do some mathematical problems." I
thought of that quiet hour last evening—perhaps it
would be quiet today as well.

O glanced at R-13, then at me with clear, round
eyes. Her cheeks flushed faintly with the delicate,
exciting hue of our coupons.

"But today I ... Today I am assigned to him,"
she nodded at R, "and in the evening he is busy.
... So that ..."

R's wet, lacquered lips mumbled good-humored-
ly "Oh, half an hour will be enough for us.
Right, O? I don't care for your problems, let's
go up to my place for a while."

I was afraid to remain alone with myself, or
rather, with that new, foreign being who merely by
some odd chance had my number—D-503. And I
went with them to R's place. True, he is not
precise, not rhythmical, he has a kind of inside-out,
mocking logic; nevertheless, we are friends. Three
years ago we had chosen together the charming,
rosy O. This bound us even more firmly than our
school years.

Then, up in R's room. Everything would seem
to be exactly the same as mine: the Table, the
glass chairs, the closet, the bed. But the moment R
entered, he moved one chair, another—and all
planes became displaced, everything slipped out of

the established proportions, became non-Euclidean. R is the same as ever. In Taylor and in mathematics he was always at the bottom of the class.

We recalled old Plapa, the little notes of thanks we boys would paste all over his glass legs (we were very fond of him). We reminisced about our law instructor.* This instructor had an extraordinarily powerful voice; it was as though blasts of violent wind blew from the loud-speaker—and we children yelled the texts after him in deafening chorus. We also recalled how the unruly R-13 once stuffed his speaker with chewed-up paper, and every text came with a shot of a spitball. R was punished, of course; what he had done was bad, of course, but now we laughed heartily—our whole triangle—and I confess, I did too.

"What if he had been alive, like the ancient teachers, eh? Wouldn't that have been ..."—a spray of words from the thick lips.

Sunlight—through the ceiling, the walls; sun—from above, from the sides, reflected from below. O sat on R's lap, and tiny drops of sunlight gleamed in her blue eyes. I felt warmed, somehow, restored. The $\sqrt{-1}$ died down, did not stir. ...

"And how is your *Integral?* We shall soon be setting off to educate the inhabitants of other planets, eh? You'd better rush it, or else we poets will turn out so much material that even your *Integral* will not be able to lift it. Every day from eight to eleven ..." R shook his head, scratched it. The back of his head is like a square little valise, attached from behind (I recalled the ancient painting, "In the Carriage").

"Are you writing for the *Integral,* too?" I was interested. "What about? Today, for example?"

---

* Naturally, his subject was not "Religious Law," or "God's Law," as the ancients called it, but the law of the One State.

"Today, about nothing. I was busy with something else ..." His 'b's spurted out at me.

"What?"

R made a grimace. "What, what! Well, if you wish, a court sentence. I versified a sentence. An idiot, one of our poets, too. .... For two years he sat next to me, and everything seemed all right. Then suddenly, how do you do! 'I am a genius,' he says, 'a genius, above the law.' And scribbled such a mess. .... Eh! Better not speak about it. ...."

The thick lips hung loosely, the lacquer vanished from his eyes. R-13 jumped up, turned, and stared somewhere through the wall. I looked at his tightly locked little valise, thinking, What is he turning over there, in that little box of his?

A moment of awkward, asymmetrical silence. It was unclear to me what the trouble was, but something was wrong.

"Fortunately, the antediluvian ages of all those Shakespeares and Dostoyevskys, or whatever you call them, are gone," I said, deliberately loudly.

R turned his face to me. The words still rushed out of him like spray, but it seemed to me that the merry shine was no longer in his eyes.

"Yes, my dearest mathematician, fortunately, fortunately, fortunately! We are the happiest arithmetical mean. .... As you mathematicians say —intergration from zero to infinity, from a cretin to Shakespeare ... yes!"

I do not know why—it seemed completely irrelevant—but I recalled the other one, her tone; the finest thread seemed to extend from her to R. (What was it?) Again the $\sqrt{-1}$ began to stir. I opened my badge—it was twenty-five minutes to seventeen. They had forty-five minutes left for their pink coupon.

"Well, I must go. ...." I kissed O, shook hands with R, and went out to the elevator.

In the street, when I had already crossed to the other side, I glanced back: in the bright, sun-permeated glass hulk of the building squares of bluish-gray, opaque drawn shades could be seen here and there—squares of rhythmic, Taylorized happiness. On the seventh floor I found R-13's square; he had already drawn the blind.

Dear O ... Dear R ... In him there is also (I don't know why "also," but let my hand write as it will) —in him there is also something not entirely clear to me. And yet, he, I, and O—we are a triangle, perhaps not equilateral, but a triangle nonetheless. To put it in the language of our ancestors (perhaps, my planetary readers, this language is more comprehensible to you), we are a family. And it is so good occasionally, if only briefly, to relax, to rest, to enclose yourself in a simple, strong triangle from all that ...

Ninth Entry

TOPICS: Liturgy
Iambics and Trochees
A Cast-Iron Hand

A bright, solemn day. On such days you forget your weaknesses, imprecisions, ailments, and everything is crystal, immutable, eternal—like our glass.

The Cube Plaza. Sixty-six great concentric circles of stands. Sixty-six rows of quiet luminous faces, eyes reflecting the glow of the sky, or perhaps the glow of the One State. Blood-red flowers—the women's lips. Tender garlands of childish faces in the front rows, near the center of action. Absorbed, stern, Gothic silence.

According to the descriptions that have come down to us, something similar was experienced by the ancients during their "religious services." But they worshiped their own irrational, unknown God; we serve our rational and precisely known one. Their God gave them nothing except eternal, tormenting searching; their God had not been able to think of anything more sensible than offering himself as sacrifice for some incomprehensible reason. We, on the other hand, offer a sacrifice to our God, the One State—a calm, reasoned, sensible sacrifice. Yes, this was our solemn liturgy to the One State, a remembrance of the awesome time of trial, of the Two Hundred Years' War, a grandiose celebration of the victory of *all* over *one*, of the *sum* over the *individual*.

The *one*. He stood on the steps of the sun-filled Cube. A white—no, not even white, already colorless—face: a glass face, glass lips. And only the eyes—black, greedy, engulfing holes. And the dread world from which he was but minutes away. The golden badge with his number had already been removed. His arms were bound with a purple ribbon—an ancient custom. (It evidently dates back to olden times, before such things were done in the name of the One State; in those days, the condemned understandably felt that they had the right to resist, and so their hands were usually bound in chains.)

And all the way above, upon the Cube, near the Machine—the motionless figure, as if cast in metal, of Him whom we call the Benefactor. His face could not be seen in detail from below; all you could tell was that it was defined in square, austere, majestic contours. But the hands ... It sometimes happens in photographs that the hands, placed in the foreground too near the camera, come out huge; they hold the eye and shut out all the rest. So with these heavy hands, still calmly reposing on the knees. And it was clear—they were stone, and the knees were barely able to support their weight.

Then suddenly one of those huge hands slowly rose—a slow, cast-iron movement. And from the stands, obeying the raised hand, a number approached the Cube. He was one of the State Poets, whose happy lot it was to crown the celebration with his verse. Divine, brass iambics thundered over the stands—about the madman with glass eyes, who stood there on the steps, awaiting the logical results of his mad ravings.

A blazing fire. In the iambics buildings swayed, went up in jets of liquid gold, collapsed. Fresh green trees withered, shriveled, sap dripping out— nothing remaining but the black crosses of their skeletons. But now Prometheus (meaning us) appeared.

> "He harnessed fire in the machine, in steel,
> And bound chaos in the chains of Law."

And everything was new, everything was steel—a steel sun, steel trees, steel men. But suddenly a madman "unchained the fire" and everything would perish again. . . .

Unfortunately, I have a poor memory for verses, but I remember one thing: it would have been impossible to choose more beautiful, more instructive images.

Again the slow, heavy gesture, and a second poet appeared on the steps of the Cube. I even rose a little from my seat: it could not be! No, those were his thick lips, it was he. . . . Why hadn't he told me he was to have this high . . . His lips trembled, they were gray. I understood: to appear before the Benefactor, before the entire host of Guardians . . . Yet— to be so nervous . . .

Sharp, quick trochees—like blows of an ax. About a heinous crime, about sacrilegious verses which dared to call the Benefactor . . . no, my hand refuses to repeat it.

R-13 sank into his seat, pale, looking at no one (I would not have expected him to be so shy). For the smallest fraction of a second I had a glimpse of someone's face—a dark, sharp, pointed triangle— flashing near him, then vanishing at once. My eyes, thousands of eyes, turned up to the Machine. The third castiron gesture of the nonhuman hand. And the transgressor, swayed by an unseen wind, walked slowly up one stair, another, and now—the last step in his life, and he is on his last bed, face to the sky, head thrown back.

The Benefactor, heavy, stony as fate, walked around the Machine, placed His huge hand on the lever. ... Not a sound, not a breath—all eyes were on that hand. What a fiery gust of exaltation one must feel to be the instrument, the resultant of a hundred thousand wills! What a great destiny!

An infinite second. The hand moved down, switching on the current. A flash of the intolerably dazzling blade of the ray, sharp as a shiver; faint crackling of the tubes in the Machine. The prone body enveloped in a light, glowing mist—and melting, melting before our eyes, dissolving with appalling speed. Then nothing—only a small puddle of chemically pure water, which but a moment ago had pulsed redly, wildly in the heart. ...

All this was elementary and known to everyone: yes, dissociation of matter; yes, splitting of the atoms of the human body. And yet each time it was a miracle—a token of the superhuman power of the Benefactor.

Above us, facing Him, the flushed faces of ten female numbers, lips parted with excitement, flowers swaying in the wind.*

According to the old custom, ten women garlanded with flowers the Benefactor's unif, still wet with spray. With the majestic step of a high priest, He slowly descended and slowly walked between

---

* From the Botanical Museum, of course. Personally, I see nothing beautiful in flowers, or in anything belonging to the primitive world long exiled beyond the Green Wall. Only the rational and useful is beautiful: machines, boots, formulas, food, and so on.

the stands. And in His wake, the delicate white branches of female hands raised high, and a million-voiced storm of cheers, shouted in unison. Then cheers in honor of the host of Guardians, invisibly present somewhere here, within our ranks. Who knows, perhaps it was precisely these Guardians who had been foreseen by the imagination of ancient man when he created his dread and gentle "archangels" assigned to each man from his birth.

Yes, there was something of the old religions, something purifying like a storm, in that solemn ceremony. You who will read this—are you familiar with such moments? I pity you if you are not. . . .

TOPICS: A Letter
A Membrane
My Shaggy Self

Yesterday was to me like the paper through which chemists filter their solutions: all suspended particles, all that is superfluous remains on this paper. And this morning I went downstairs freshly distilled, transparent.

Downstairs in the vestibule, the controller sat at her table, glancing at the watch and writing down the numbers of those who entered. Her name is U ... but I had better not mention her number, lest I say something unflattering about her. Although, essentially, she is quite a respectable middle-aged woman. The only thing I dislike about her is that her cheeks sag like the gills of a fish (but why should that disturb me?).

Her pen scraped, and I saw myself on the page—D-503, and next to me an inkblot.

I was just about to draw her attention to it when she raised her head and dripped an inky little smile at me. "There is a letter for you. Yes. You will get it, my dear, yes, yes, you will get it."

I know that the letter, which she had read, still

had to pass the Office of the Guardians (I believe there is no need to explain to you this natural procedure), and would reach me not later than twelve. But I was disturbed by that little smile; the ink drop muddied my transparent solution. So much, in fact, that later, at the *Integral* construction site, I could not concentrate and even made a mistake in my calculations, which had never happened to me before.

At twelve, again the pinkish-brown gills, and finally the letter was in my hands. I don't know why I did not read it at once, but slipped it into my pocket and hurried to my room. I opened it, ran through it, and sat down. ... It was an official notification that number I-330 had registered for me and that I was to be at her room today at twenty-one. The address was given below.

No! After everything that had happened, after I had so unequivocally shown my feelings toward her! Besides, she did not even know whether I had gone to the Office of the Guardians. After all, she had no way of learning that I had been sick—well, that I generally could not ... And despite all this ...

A dynamo whirled, hummed in my head. Buddha, yellow silk, lilies of the valley, a rosy crescent ... Oh, yes, and this too: O was to visit me today. Ought I to show her the notice concerning I-330? I didn't know. She would not believe (indeed, how could she?) that I've had nothing to do with it, that I was entirely ... And I was sure—there would be a difficult, senseless, absolutely illogical conversation ... No, only not that. Let everything be resolved automatically: I would simply send her a copy of the notice.

I hurriedly stuffed the notice into my pocket—and suddenly saw this dreadful, apelike hand of mine. I recalled how I-330 had taken my hand that time, during the walk, and looked at it. Did she really ...

And then it was a quarter to twenty-one. A white night. Everything seemed made of greenish glass. But a very different glass from ours—fragile, unreal, a thin glass shell; and under it something whirling, rushing, humming ... And I would not have been astonished if the cupolas of the auditoriums had risen up in slow, round clouds of smoke, and the elderly moon smiled inkily—like the woman at the table in the morning, and all the shades dropped suddenly in all the houses, and behind the shades ...

A strange sensation: I felt as though my ribs were iron rods, constricting, definitely constricting my heart—there was not room enough for it. I stood before the glass door with the golden figures: I-330. She was sitting with her back to me, at the table, writing something. I entered.

"Here ..." I held out the pink coupon. "I was notified today, and so I came."

"How prompt you are! One moment, may I? Sit down, I'll just finish."

Again her eyes turned down to the letter—and what was going on within her, behind those lowered shades? What would she say? What was I to do a minute later? How could I find out, how calculate it, when all of her was—from *there*, from the savage, ancient land of dreams?

I looked at her silently. My ribs were iron rods; I could not breathe ... When she spoke, her face was like a rapid, sparkling wheel—you could not see the individual spokes. But now the wheel was motionless. And I saw a strange combination: dark eyebrows raised high at the temples—a mocking, sharp triangle. And yet another, pointing upward—the two deep lines from the corners of her mouth to the nose. And these two triangles somehow contradicted one another, stamped the entire face with an unpleasant, irritating X, like a slanting cross. A face marked with a cross.

The wheel began to turn, the spokes ran together. . . .

"So you did not go to the Office of the Guardians?"

"I did not . . . could not—I was sick."

"Certainly. I thought so. Something had to prevent you—no matter what." (Sharp teeth, smile.) "But now you are in my hands. You remember—'Every number who has failed to report to the Office of the Guardians within forty-eight hours, is considered . . .' "

My heart thumped so violently that the rods bent. Caught stupidly, like a boy. And stupidly I kept silent. And I felt: I'm trapped, I cannot move a hand or a foot.

She stood up and stretched lazily. Then she pressed a button, and the shades dropped, crackling lightly. I was cut off from the world, alone with her.

I-330 was somewhere behind me, near the closet. Her unif rustled, fell. I listened, all of me listened. And I remembered . . . no, it flashed upon me within one hundredth of a second . . .

I had had occasion recently to calculate the curve for a street membrane of a new type (now these membranes, gracefully camouflaged, were installed on every street, recording all conversations for the Office of the Guardians). And I remembered the rosy, concave, quivering film, the strange creature consisting of a single organ—an ear. I was such a membrane at this moment.

A click of the fastening at the collar, on the breast, still lower. The glass silk rustled down the shoulders, knees, dropped to the floor. I heard, more clearly than I could see, one foot step out of the bluish-gray silk pile, the other. ...

The tautly stretched membrane quivered and recorded silence. No: sharp blows of a hammer against the iron rods, with endless pauses. And I heard—I saw her behind me, thinking for a second.

And now—the closet doors, the click of an opening lid—and again silk, silk ...

"Well, if you please."

I turned. She was in a light, saffron-yellow dress of the ancient model. This was a thousand times more cruel than if she had worn nothing. Two pointed tips through the filmy silk, glowing pink—two embers through the ash. Two delicately rounded knees ...

She sat in a low armchair. On the rectangular table before her, a bottle with something poisonously green, two tiny glasses on stems. At the corner of her lips a thread of smoke—that ancient smoking substance in the finest paper tube (I forget what it was called).

The membrane still quivered. The hammer pounded inside me against the red-hot iron rods. I clearly heard each blow, and ... and suddenly: What if she heard it too?

But she puffed calmly, glancing at me calmly, and carelessly shook off the ash—on my pink coupon.

As coolly as I could, I asked, "Now, listen, if that's the case, why did you register for me? And why did you compel me to come here?"

It was as if she did not hear. She poured the liquid from the bottle into her glass, sipped it.

"Delicious liqueur. Would you like some?"

It was only now that I understood: alcohol. Yesterday's scene flashed like a stroke of lightning: the Benefactor's stony hand, the blinding ray. But on the Cube above—*this* body, prostrate, with the head thrown back. I shuddered.

"Listen," I said. "You know that everyone who poisons himself with nicotine, and especially alcohol, is ruthlessly destroyed by the One State. . . ."

Dark eyebrows rose high to the temples, a sharp mocking triangle. "Quick destruction of a few is more sensible than giving many the opportunity to ruin themselves? And then, degeneration, and so on. Right—to the point of indecency."

"Yes . . . to the point of indecency."

"And if this little company of naked, bald truths were to be let out in the street . . . No, just imagine. . . . Well, take the most constant admirer of mine—oh, but you know him. . . . Imagine that he has discarded all the falsehood of clothes and stood among the people in his true shape. . . . Oh!"

She laughed. But I could clearly see her lower, sorrowful triangle—the two deep lines from the corners of her mouth to her nose. And for some reason these lines revealed it to me: that stooping, wing-eared, doubly curved . . . he embraced her—as she was now. . . . He . . .

But I am trying to convey the feelings—the abnormal feelings—I had at that moment. Now, as I write this, I am perfectly aware that all of this is as it should be. Like every honest number, he has an equal right to joy, and it would be unjust . . . Oh, well, but this is clear.

I-330 laughed very strangely and very long. Then she looked closely at me—into me. "But the main thing is that I am completely at ease with you. You are such a dear—oh, I am sure of it—you will never think of going to the Office and reporting that I drink liqueur, that I smoke. You will be sick, or you will be busy, or whatever. I am even sure that in a moment you will drink this marvelous poison with me. . . ."

That brazen, mocking tone. I definitely felt: now I hate her again. But why the "now"? I have hated her all the time.

She tilted the whole glassful of green poison into her mouth, stood up, and, glowing pink through the transparent saffron, took several steps ... and stopped behind my chair.

Suddenly, an arm around my neck, lips into lips—no, somewhere still deeper, still more terrifying. I swear, this took me completely by surprise, and perhaps that was the only reason why ... After all, I could not—now I realize it clearly—I myself could not have wanted what happened after that.

Intolerably sweet lips (I suppose it must have been the taste of the "liqueur")—and a mouthful of fiery poison flowed into me—then more, and more. ... I broke away from the earth and, like a separate planet, whirling madly, rushed down, down, along an unknown, uncalculated orbit. ...

What followed can be described only approximately, only by more or less close analogies.

It has never occurred to me before, but this is truly how it is: all of us on earth walk constantly over a seething, scarlet sea of flame, hidden below, in the belly of the earth. We never think of it. But what if the thin crust under our feet should turn into glass and we should suddenly see ...

I became glass. I saw—within myself.

There were two of me. The former one, D-503, number D-503, and the other ... Before, he had just barely shown his hairy paws from within the shell; now all of him broke out, the shell cracked; a moment, and it would fly to pieces and ... And then ... what?

With all my strength, as though clutching at a straw, I gripped the arms of the chair and asked—only to hear myself, the other self, the old one,

"Where . . . where did you get this . . . this poison?"

"Oh, this! A certain doctor, one of my . . ."

" 'One of my . . .'? 'One of my'—what?" And suddenly the other leaped out and yelled, "I won't allow it! I want no one but me. I'll kill anyone who . . . Because I . . . Because you . . . I . . ."

I saw—he seized her roughly with his shaggy paws, tore the silk, and sank his teeth into . . . I remember exactly—his teeth . . .

I don't know how, but I-330 managed to slip away. And now—her eyes behind that damned impermeable shade—she stood leaning with her back against the wardrobe and listened to me.

I remember—I was on the floor, embracing her legs, kissing her knees, pleading, "Now, right this minute, right now . . ."

Sharp teeth, sharp mocking triangle of eyebrows. She bent down and silently unpinned my badge.

"Yes! Yes, darling, darling." I hurriedly began to throw off my unif. But I-330 just as silently showed me the watch on my badge. It was five minutes to twenty-two and a half.

I turned cold. I knew what it meant to be seen in the street after twenty-two and a half. My madness vanished as if blown away. I was myself. And one thing was clear to me: I hate her, hate her, hate her!

Without a good-by, without a backward glance, I rushed out of the room. Hurriedly pinning on the badge as I ran, skipping steps, down the stairway (afraid of meeting someone in the elevator), I burst out into the empty street.

Everything was in its usual place—so simple, ordinary, normal: the glass houses gleaming with lights, the pale glass sky, the motionless greenish night. But under this cool quiet glass something violent, blood-red, shaggy, rushed soundlessly. And I raced, gasping, not to be late.

57

Suddenly I felt the hastily pinned badge loosening—it slipped off, clicking on the glass pavement. I bent down to pick it up, and in the momentary silence heard the stamping of feet behind me. I turned—something little, bowed, slunk out from around the corner, or so it seemed to me at the time.

I rushed on at full speed, the air whistling in my ears. At the entrance I stopped: the watch showed one minute before twenty-two and a half. I listened—there was no one behind me. Obviously, it had all been a preposterous fantasy, the effect of the poison.

It was a night of torment. My bed rose and sank and rose again under me, floating along a sinusoid. I argued with myself: At night numbers must sleep; it is their duty, just as it is their duty to work in the daytime. Not sleeping at night is a criminal offense. ... And yet, I could not and could not.

I am perishing. I am unable to fulfill my obligations to the One State. ... I ...

Eleventh Entry

TOPICS: No, I cannot, I'll simply write, without a plan

Evening. A light mist. The sky is hidden by a milky-golden veil and you cannot see what is above, beyond it. The ancients knew that God—their greatest, bored skeptic—was there. We know that there is only a crystal-blue, naked, indecent nothing. But now I do not know what is there: I have learned too much. Knowledge, absolutely sure of its infallibility, is faith. I had had firm faith in myself; I had believed that I knew everything within myself. And now . . .

I stand before a mirror. And for the first time in my life—yes, for the first time—I see myself clearly, sharply, consciously. I see myself with astonishment as a certain "he." Here am I—he: black eyebrows, etched in a straight line; and between them, like a scar, a vertical fold (I don't know whether it was there before). Steel-gray eyes, surrounded by the shadow of a sleepless night. And there, behind this steel . . . it turns out that I have never known what is there. And out of "there" (this "there" is at the same time here and infinitely far), out of "there" I look at myself—at him—and I know: he, with his straight eyebrows, is a stranger, alien to me, someone I am meeting for the first time in my life. And I, the real I, am not he.

No. Period. All this is nonsense, and all these absurd sensations are but delirium, the result of yesterday's poisoning. . . . Poisoning by what?—a sip of the green venom, or by her? It does not matter. I am writing all this down merely to show how strangely human reason, so sharp and so precise, can be confused and thrown into disarray. Reason that had succeeded in making even infinity, of which the ancients were so frightened, acceptable to them by means of . . .

The annunciator clicks: it is R-13. Let him come; in fact, I am glad. It is too difficult for me to be alone now. . . .

Twenty minutes later

On the plane surface of the paper, in the two-dimensional world, these lines are next to one another. But in a different world they . . . I am losing my sense of figures: twenty minutes may be two hundred or two hundred thousand. And it seems so strange to write down in calm, measured, carefully chosen words what has occurred just now between me and R. It is like sitting down in an armchair by your own bedside, legs crossed, and watching curiously how you yourself are writhing in the bed.

When R-13 entered, I was perfectly calm and normal. I spoke with sincere admiration of how splendidly he had succeeded in versifying the sentence, and told him that his trochees had been the most effective instrument of all in crushing and destroying that madman.

60

"I would even say—if I were asked to draw up a schematic blueprint of the Benefactor's Machine, I would somehow, somehow find a way of incorporating your verses into the drawing," I concluded.

But suddenly I noticed R's eyes turn lusterless, his lips turn gray.

"What is it?"

"What, what! Oh ... Oh, I'm simply tired of it. Everyone around talks of nothing but the sentence. I don't want to hear about it any more. I just don't want to!"

He frowned and rubbed the back of his head—that little box of his with its strange baggage that I did not understand. A pause. And then he found something in the box, pulled it out, opened it. His eyes glossed over with laughter as he jumped up.

"But for your *Integral*, I am composing ... That will be ... Oh, yes, that will be something!"

It was again the old R: thick, sputtering lips, spraying saliva, and a fountain of words. "You see" ("s"—a spray) ". . . that ancient legend about paradise ... Why, it's about us, about today. Yes! Just think. Those two, in paradise, were given a choice: happiness without freedom, or freedom without happiness. There was no third alternative. Those idiots chose freedom, and what came of it? Of course, for ages afterward they longed for the chains. The chains—you understand? That's what world sorrow was about. For ages! And only we have found the way of restoring happiness. ... No, wait, listen further! The ancient God and we—side by side, at the same table. Yes! We have helped God ultimately to conquer the devil—for it was he who had tempted men to break the ban and get a taste of ruinous freedom, he, the evil serpent. And we, we've brought down our boot over his little head, and—cr-runch! Now everything is fine—we have paradise again. Again we are as innocent and simple-hearted as Adam and Eve. No more of that confusion about good and evil. Everything is simple—heavenly, childishly simple. The Benefactor, the Machine, the Cube, the Gas Bell, the Guardians—all this is good, all this is sublime, magnificent, noble, elevated, crystally pure. Because it protects our unfreedom—that is, our happiness. The ancients would begin to talk and think and break their heads—ethical, unethical . . . Well, then. In short, what about such a paradisiac poem, eh? And, of course, in the most serious tone. . . . You understand? Quite something, eh?"

Understand? It was simple enough. I remember thinking: such an absurd, asymmetrical face, yet such a clear, correct mind. This is why he is so close to me, the real me (I still consider my old self the true one; all of this today is, of course, only a sickness).

R evidently read these thoughts on my face. He put his arm around my shoulders and roared with laughter.

"Ah, you . . . Adam! Yes, incidentally, about Eve . . ."

He fumbled in his pocket, took out a notebook, and turned the pages. "The day after tomorrow . . . no, in two days, O has a pink coupon to visit you. How do you feel about it? As before? Do you want her to . . ."

"Of course, naturally."

"I'll tell her so. She is a little shy herself, you see. . . . What a business! With me, it is nothing, you know, merely a pink coupon, but with you. . . . And she would not tell me who the fourth one is that broke into our triangle. Confess it now, you reprobate, who is it? Well?"

A curtain flew up inside me—the rustle of silk, a green bottle, lips. . . . And inappropriately, to no purpose, the words broke out (if I had only restrained myself!) : "Tell me, have you ever tasted nicotine or alcohol?"

R compressed his lips and threw me a sidelong look. I heard his thoughts with utmost clarity: You may be a friend, all right . . . still. . . . And then his answer: "Well, how shall I put it? Actually, no. But I knew a certain woman . . ."

"I-330," I shouted.

"So . . . you—you too? With her?" He filled with laughter, gulped, ready to spill over.

My mirror hung on the wall in such a way that I could see myself only across the table; from here, from the chair, I saw only my forehead and my eyebrows.

And now I—the real I—saw in the mirror the twisted, jumping line of eyebrows, and the real I heard a wild, revolting shout: "What 'too'? What do you mean, 'too'? No, I demand an answer!"

Gaping thick lips, bulging eyes. Then I—the real I—seized the other, the wild, shaggy, panting one, by the scruff of the neck. The real I said to R, "Forgive me, for the Benefactor's sake. I am quite ill, I cannot sleep. I don't know what is happening to me . . ."

A fleeting smile on the thick lips. "Yes, yes! I understand, I understand! It's all familiar to me . . . theoretically, of course. Good-by!"

In the doorway he turned, bounced back toward me like a small black ball, and threw a book down on the table.

"My latest . . . I brought it for you—almost forgot it. Good-by . . ." The "b" sprayed at me, and he rolled out of the room.

I am alone. Or, rather, alone with that other "I." I am sitting in the chair, legs crossed, watching with curiosity from some "there" how I—my own self—writhe in the bed.

Why, why is it that for three whole years O and

R and I have had that fine, warm friendship, and now—a single word about the other one, about I-330 ... Is it possible that all this madness—love, jealousy—exists not only in those idiotic ancient books? And to think that I ... Equations, formulas, figures, and ... this! I don't understand anything ... anything at all. ... Tomorrow I shall go to R and tell him that ...

No, it isn't true, I will not go. Neither tomorrow, nor the day after tomorrow—I shall never go. I cannot, I don't want to see him. It is the end! Our triangle is broken.

I am alone. Evening. A light mist. The sky is hidden behind a milky-golden veil. If only I could know what is there, above it! If only I could know: Who am I, what am I like?

Twelfth Entry

I have the constant feeling: I will recover, I can recover. I slept very well. None of those dreams or other morbid symptoms. Tomorrow dear O will come to me, and everything will be as simple, right, and limited as a circle. I do not fear this word "limitation." The function of man's highest faculty, his reason, consists precisely of the continuous limitation of infinity, the breaking up of infinity into convenient, easily digestible portions—differentials. This is precisely what lends my field, mathematics, its divine beauty. And it is the understanding of this beauty that the other one, I-330, lacks. However, this is merely in passing—a chance association.

All these thoughts—in time to the measured, regular clicking of the wheels of the underground train. I silently scanned the rhythm of the wheels and R's poems (from the book he had given me yesterday). Then I became aware of someone cautiously bending over my shoulder from behind and peering at the opened page. Without turning, out of the merest corner of my eye, I saw the pink wide wing-ears, the double-bent . . . it was he! Reluctant to disturb him, I pretended not to notice. I cannot imagine how he got there; he did not seem to be in the car when I entered.

This incident, trivial in itself, had a particularly pleasant effect upon me; it strengthened me. How good it is to know that a vigilant eye is fixed upon you, lovingly protecting you against the slightest error, the slightest misstep. This may seem somewhat sentimental, but an analogy comes to my mind—the Guardian Angels that the ancients dreamed of. How many of the things they merely dreamed about have been realized in our life!

At the moment when I felt the Guardian Angel behind my back, I was enjoying a sonnet entitled "Happiness." I think I will not be mistaken if I say that it is a poem of rare and profound beauty of thought. Here are its first four lines:

> Eternally enamored two times two,
> Eternally united in the passionate four,
> Most ardent lovers in the world—
> Inseparable two times two . . .

And so on—about the wise, eternal bliss of the multiplication table.

Every true poet is inevitably a Columbus. America existed for centuries before Columbus, but only Columbus succeeded in discovering it. The multiplication table existed for centuries before R-13, yet it was only R-13 who found a new Eldorado in the virginal forest of figures. And indeed, is there any happiness wiser, more unclouded than the happiness of this miraculous world? Steel rusts. The ancient God created the old man, capable of erring—hence he erred himself. The multiplication able is wiser and more absolute than the ancient

God: it never—do you realize the full meaning of the word?—it never errs. And there are no happier figures than those which live according to the harmonious, eternal laws of the multiplication table. No hesitations, no delusions. There is only one truth, and only one true way; this truth is two times two, and the true way—four. And would it not be an absurdity if these happily, ideally multiplied twos began to think of some nonsensical freedom—i.e., clearly, to error? To me it is axiomatic that R-13 succeeded in grasping the most fundamental, the most . . .

At this point I felt once more—first at the back of my head, then at my left ear—the warm, delicate breath of my Guardian Angel. He had obviously noticed that the book on my lap was now closed and my thoughts far away. Well, I was ready, there and then, to open all the pages of my mind to him; there was such serenity, such joy in this feeling. I remember: I turned and looked into his eyes with pleading insistence, but he did not understand, or did not wish to understand, and asked me nothing. Only one thing remains to me—to speak to you, my unknown readers, about everything. (At this moment you are as dear and near and unattainable to me as he was then.)

My reflections proceeded from the part to the whole: the part, R-13; the majestic whole, our Institute of State Poets and Writers. I wondered at the ancients who had never realized the utter absurdity of their literature and poetry. The enormous, magnificent power of the literary word was completely wasted. It's simply ridiculous—everyone wrote anything he pleased. Just as ridiculous and absurd as the fact that the ancients allowed the ocean to beat dully at the shore twenty-four hours a day, while the millions of kilogrammometers of energy residing in the waves went only to heighten lovers' feelings. But we have extracted electricity from the amorous whisper of the waves; we have transformed the savage, foam-spitting beast into a domestic animal; and in the same way we have tamed and harnessed the once wild element of poetry. Today, poetry is no longer the idle, impudent whistling of a nightingale; poetry is civic service, poetry is useful.

Take, for example, our famous "mathematical couplets." Could we have learned in school to love the four rules of arithmetic so tenderly and so sincerely without them? Or "Thorns," that classical image: the Guardians as the thorns on the rose, protecting the delicate flower of the State from rude contacts. . . . Whose heart can be so stony as to remain unmoved at the sight of innocent childish lips reciting like a prayer the verse:

> "The bad boy rudely sniffed the rose,
> But the steely thorn pricked his nose.
> The mischief-maker cries, 'Oh, Oh,'
> And runs as fast as he can go," and so on.

Or the *Daily Odes to the Benefactor*? Who, upon reading them, will not bow piously before the selfless labors of this Number of Numbers? Or the awesome *Red Flowers of Court Sentences*? Or the immortal tragedy *He Who Was Late to Work*? Or the guidebook *Stanzas on Sexual Hygiene*?

All of our life, in its entire complexity and beauty, has been engraved forever in the gold of words.

Our poets no longer soar in the empyrean; they have come down to earth; they stride beside us to the stern mechanical March of the Music Plant. Their lyre encompasses the morning scraping of electric toothbrushes and the dread crackle of the sparks in the Benefactor's Machine; the majestic echoes of the Hymn to the One State and the intimate tinkle of the gleaming crystal chamber-pot; the exciting rustle of dropping shades, the merry voices of the latest cookbook, and the scarcely audible whisper of the listening membranes in the streets.

Our gods are here, below, with us—in the office, the kitchen, the workshop, the toilet; the gods have become like us. Ergo, we have become as gods, And we shall come to you, my unknown readers on the distant planet, to make your life as divinely rational and precise as ours.

Thirteenth Entry

TOPICS: Fog
Thou
An Utterly Absurd Incident

I woke at dawn; the solid, rosy firmament greeted my eyes. Everything was beautifully round. In the evening O would be here. I felt: I am completely well. I smiled and fell asleep again.

The morning bell. I rose. But now all was different around me: through the glass of the ceiling, the wall—everywhere—dense, penetrating fog. Crazy clouds, now heavier, now lighter. There were no longer any boundaries between sky and earth; everything was flying, melting, falling—nothing to get hold of. No more houses. The glass walls dissolved in the fog like salt crystals in water. From the street, the dark figures inside the houses were like particles suspended in a milky, nightmare solution, some hanging low, some higher and still higher—all the way up to the tenth floor. And everything was swirling smoke, as in a silent, raging fire.

Exactly eleven-forty-five; I glanced deliberately at the watch—to grasp at the figures, at the solid safety of the figures.

At eleven-forty-five, before going to perform the

usual physical labor prescribed by the Table of Hours, I stopped off for a moment in my room. Suddenly, the telephone rang. The voice—a long, slow needle plunged into the heart: "Ah, you are still home? I am glad. Wait for me on the corner. We shall go ... you'll see where."

"You know very well that I am going to work now."

"You know very well that you will do as I tell you. Good-by. In two minutes ..."

Two minutes later I stood on the corner. After all, I had to prove to her that I was governed by the One State, not by her. "You will do as I tell you ..." And so sure of herself—I could hear it in her voice. Well, now I shall have a proper talk with her.

Gray unifs, woven of the raw, damp fog, hurriedly came into being at my side and instantly dissolved in the fog. I stared at my watch, all of me a sharp, quivering second hand. Eight minutes, ten ... Three minutes to twelve, two minutes ...

Finished. I was already late for work. I hated her. But I had to prove to her ...

At the corner, through the white fog, blood—a slit, as with a sharp knife—her lips.

"I am afraid I delayed you. But then, it's all the same. It is too late for you now."

How I ... But she was right, it was too late.

I silently stared at her lips. All women are lips, nothing but lips. Some pink, firmly round—a ring, a tender protection against the whole world. But these: a second ago they did not exist, and now—a knife slit—and the sweet blood will drip down.

She moved nearer, leaned her shoulder against me—and we were one, and something flowed from her into me, and I knew: this is how it must be. I knew it with every nerve, and every hair, every heartbeat, so sweet it verged on pain. And what

71

joy to submit to this "must." A piece of iron must feel such joy as it submits to the precise, inevitable law that draws it to a magnet. Or a stone, thrown up, hesitating a moment, then plunging headlong back to earth. Or a man, after the final agony, taking a last deep breath—and dying.

I remember I smiled dazedly and said, for no good reason, "Fog . . . So very . . ."

"Do you like fog?"

She used the ancient, long-forgotten "thou"—the "thou" of the master to the slave. It entered into me slowly, sharply. Yes, I was a slave, and this, too, was necessary, was good.

"Yes, good . . ." I said aloud to myself. And then to her, "I hate fog. I am afraid of it."

"That means you love it. You are afraid of it because it is stronger than you; you hate it because you are afraid of it; you love it because you cannot subdue it to your will. Only the unsubduable can be loved."

Yes, this is true. And this is precisely why— precisely why I . . .

We walked, the two of us—one. Somewhere far through the fog the sun sang almost inaudibly, everything was filling up with firmness, with pearl, gold, rose, red. The entire world was a single unencompassable woman, and we were in its very womb, unborn, ripening joyfully. And it was clear to me—ineluctably clear—that the sun, the fog, the rose, and the gold were all for me. . . .

I did not ask where we were going. It did not matter. The only thing that mattered was to walk, to walk, to ripen, to fill up more and more firmly. . . .

"Here." I-330 stopped at a door. "The one I spoke to you about at the Ancient House is on duty here today."

From far away, with my eyes only, protecting

what was ripening within me, I read the sign: MEDICAL OFFICE. I understood.

A glass room filled with golden fog. Glass ceilings, colored bottles, jars. Wires. Bluish sparks in tubes.

And a tiny man, the thinnest I had ever seen. All of him seemed cut out of paper, and no matter which way he turned, there was nothing but a profile, sharply honed: the nose a sharp blade, lips like scissors.

I did not hear what I-330 said to him: I watched her speak, and felt myself smiling blissfully, uncontrollably. The scissor-lips flashed and the doctor said, "Yes, yes. I understand. The most dangerous disease—I know of nothing more dangerous. . . ." He laughed, quickly wrote something with the thinnest of paper hands, and gave the slip to I-330; then he wrote another one and gave it to me.

He had given us certificates that we were ill and could not report to work. I was stealing my services from the One State, I was a thief, I saw myself under the Benefactor's Machine. But all of this was as remote and indifferent as a story in a book ... I took the slip without a moment's hesitation. I—all of me, my eyes, lips, hands—knew that this had to be.

At the corner, at the almost empty garage, we took an aero. I-330 sat down at the controls, as she had the first time, and switched the starter to "Forward." We broke from the earth and floated away. And everything followed us: the rosy-golden fog, the sun, the finest blade of the doctor's profile, suddenly so dear. Formerly, everything had turned around the sun; now I knew—everything was turning around me—slowly, blissfully, with tightly closed eyes. ...

The old woman at the gates of the Ancient House. The dear mouth, grown together, with its

i wrinkles. It must have been closed all these
but now it opened, smiled. "Aah, you mis-
vous imp! Instead of working like everybody
else ... oh, well, go in, go in! If anything goes
wrong, I'll come and warn you. ..."

The heavy, creaky, untransparent door closed,
and at once my heart opened painfully wide—still
wider—all the way. Her lips were mine. I drank
and drank. I broke away, stared silently into her
eyes, wide open to me, and again ...

The twilight of the rooms, the blue, the saffron-
yellow, the dark green leather, Buddha's golden
smile, the glimmering mirrors. And—my old
dream, so easy to understand now—everything
filled with golden-pink sap, ready to overflow, to
spurt. ...

It ripened. And inevitably, as iron and the magnet, in sweet submission to the exact, immutable
law, I poured myself into her. There was no pink
coupon, no accounting, no State, not even myself.
There were only the tenderly sharp clenched teeth,
the golden eyes wide open to me; and through
them I entered slowly, deeper and deeper. And
silence. Only in the corner, thousands of miles
away, drops falling in the washstand, and I was
the universe, and from one drop to the other—
eons, millennia. ...

Slipping on my unif, I bent down to I-330 and
drank her in with my eyes for the last time.

"I knew it ... I knew you ..." she said, just
audibly.

Rising quickly, she put on her unif and her
usual sharp bite-smile. "Well, fallen angel. You're
lost now. You're not afraid? Good-by, then! You
will return alone. There."

She opened the mirrored door of the wardrobe;
looking at me over her shoulder, she waited. I
went out obediently. But I had barely stepped

74

across the threshold when suddenly I felt that I must feel her press against me with her shoulder—only for a second, only with her shoulder, nothing more.

I rushed back, into the room where she was probably still fastening her unif before the mirror. I ran in—and stopped. I clearly saw the ancient key ring still swaying in the door of the wardrobe, but I-330 was not there. She could not have left—there was only one exit. And yet she was not there. I searched everywhere, I even opened the wardrobe and felt the bright, ancient dresses. No one ...

I feel embarrassed, somehow, my planetary readers, to tell you about this altogether improbable occurrence. But what can I say if this was exactly how it happened? Wasn't the whole day, from the earliest morning, full of improbabilities? Isn't it all like that ancient sickness of dreams? And if so, what difference does it make if there is one absurdity more, or one less? Besides, I am certain that sooner or later I shall succeed in fitting all these absurdities into some logical formula. This reassures me and, I hope, will reassure you.

But how full I am! If only you could know how full I am—to the very brim!

More about the other day. My personal hour before bedtime was occupied, and I could not record it yesterday. But all of it is etched in me, and most of all—perhaps forever—that intolerably cold floor. . . .

In the evening O was to come to me—this was her day. I went down to the number on duty to obtain permission to lower my shades.

"What is wrong with you?" the man on duty asked me. "You seem to be sort of . . ."

"I . . . I am not well. . . ."

As a matter of fact, it was true. I am certainly sick. All of this is an illness. And I remembered: yes, of course, the doctor's note. . . . I felt for it in my pocket—it rustled there. Then everything had really happened, it had been real. . . .

I held out the slip of paper to the man on duty. My cheeks burned. Without looking, I saw him glance up at me, surprised.

And then it was twenty-one and a half. In the room at the left, the shades were down. In the room at the right, I saw my neighbor over a book—his knobby brow and bald head a huge yellow parabola. Tormentedly I paced my room. How could I now, with O, after all that had happened? And from the right I sensed distinctly the man's eyes upon me, I saw distinctly the wrinkles on his forehead—a row of yellow illegible lines; and for some reason it seemed to me those lines were about me.

At a quarter to twenty-two a joyous rosy hurricane burst into my room, a strong circle of rosy arms closed about my neck. And then I felt the circle weakening, weakening. It broke. The arms dropped.

"You're not the same, you're not the old one, not mine!"

"What sort of primitive notion—'mine'? I never was ..." and I broke off. It came to me: it's true; before this I never was ... But now? Now I no longer live in our clear, rational world; I live in the ancient nightmare world, the world of square roots of minus one.

The shades fell. Behind the wall on the right my neighbor dropped his book on the floor, and in the last, momentary narrow slit between the shade and the floor I saw the yellow hand picking up the book, and my one wish was to grasp at that hand with all my strength. ...

"I thought—I hoped to meet you during the walk today. I have so much—there is so much I must tell you ..."

Sweet, poor O! Her rosy mouth—a rosy crescent, its horns down. But how can I tell her what happened? I cannot, if only because that would make her an accomplice to my crimes. I knew she would not have enough strength to go to the Office of the Guardians, and hence ...

She lay back. I kissed her slowly. I kissed that

plump, naïve fold on her wrist. Her blue eyes were closed, and the rosy crescent slowly opened, bloomed, and I kissed all of her.

And then I felt how empty, how drained I was— I had given everything away. I cannot, must not. I must—and it's impossible. My lips grew cold at once. . . .

The rosy half-moon trembled, wilted, twisted. O drew the blanket over herself, wrapped herself in it, hid her face in the pillow. . . .

I sat on the floor near the bed—what an incredibly cold floor!—I sat silently. The agonizing cold rose from beneath, higher and higher. It must be cold like this in the blue, silent, interplanetary space.

"But you must understand, I did not want to . . ." I muttered. "I did all I could . . ."

This was true. I, the real I, had not wanted to. And yet how could I tell her this? How explain that the iron may not want to, but the law is ineluctable, exact. . . .

O raised her face from the pillow and said without opening her eyes, "Go away." But she was crying, and the words came out as "gooway," and for some reason this silly trifle cut deeply into me.

Chilled, numb all through, I went out into the corridor. Outside, behind the glass, a light, barely visible mist. By nightfall the fog would probably be dense again. What would happen that night?

O silently slipped past me toward the elevator. The door clicked.

"One moment," I cried out, suddenly frightened.

But the elevator was already humming, down, down, down.

She had robbed me of R.

She had robbed me of O.

And yet, and yet . . .

Fifteenth Entry

TOPICS: The Bell
The Mirror-Smooth Sea
I Am to Burn Eternally

I had just stepped into the dock where the *Integral* is being built when the Second Builder hurried to meet me. His face—round, white, as usual—a china plate; and his words, like something exquisitely tasty, served up on the plate: "Well, while it pleased you to be sick the other day, we had, I'd say, quite a bit of excitement here in the chief's absence."

"Excitement?"

"Oh, yes! The bell rang at the end of the workday, and everybody began to file out. And imagine—the doorman caught a man without a number. I'll never understand how he managed to get in. He was taken to the Operational Section. They'll know how to drag the why and how out of the fellow . . ." (All this with the tastiest smile.)

The Operational Section is staffed with our best and most experienced physicians, who work under the direct supervision of the Benefactor Himself. They have a variety of instruments, the most effective of them all the famous Gas Bell. Essentially, it is the old school laboratory experiment: a mouse is placed under a glass jar and an air pump gradually rarefies the air inside it. And so on. But, of course, the Gas Bell is a much more perfect apparatus, using all sorts of gases. And then, this is no longer torture of a tiny helpless animal. It serves a noble end: it safeguards the security of the One State—in other words, the happiness of millions. About five centuries ago, when the Operational Section was first being developed, there were some fools who compared the Section to the ancient Inquisition, but that is as absurd as equating a surgeon performing a tracheotomy with a highwayman; both may have the same knife in their hands, both do the same thing—cut a living man's throat—yet one is a benefactor, the other a criminal; one has a $+$ sign, the other a $-$.

All this is entirely clear—within a single second, at a single turn of the logical machine. Then suddenly the gears catch on the minus, and something altogether different comes to ascendancy—the key ring, still swaying in the door. The door had evidently just been shut, yet I-330 was already gone, vanished. That was something the machine could not digest in any way. A dream? But even now I felt that strange sweet pain in my right shoulder—I-330 pressing herself against the shoulder, next to me in the fog. "Do you like fog?" Yes, I love the fog. . . . I love everything, and everything is firm, new, astonishing, everything is good. . . .

"Everything is good," I said aloud.

"Good?" The china eyes goggled at me. "What is good about this? If that unnumbered one had managed . . . it means that they are everywhere, all around us, at all times . . . they are here, around the *Integral,* they . . ."

"Who are *they?*"

"How would I know who? But I feel them, you understand? All the time."

"And have you heard about the newly invented operation—excision of the imagination?" (I had myself heard something of the kind a few days earlier.)

"I know about it. But what has that to do with . . . ?"

"Just this: in your place, I would go and ask to be operated on."

Something distinctly lemon-sour appeared on the plate. The good fellow was offended by the hint that he might possibly possess imagination. . . . Oh, well, only a week ago I would have been offended myself. Not today. Today I know that I have it, that I am ill. I also know that I don't want to be cured. I don't, and that's all there is to it. We ascended the glass stairs. Everything below was as clearly visible as if it were spread out on the palm of my hand.

You, who read these notes, whoever you may be—you have a sun over your heads. And if you have ever been as ill as I am now, you know what the sun is like—what it can be like—in the morning. You know that pink, transparent, warm gold, when the very air is faintly rosy and everything is suffused with the delicate blood of the sun, everything is alive: the stones are alive and soft; iron is alive and soft; people are alive, and everyone is smiling. In an hour, all this may vanish, in an hour the rosy blood may trickle out, but for the moment everything lives. And I see something pulsing and flowing in the glass veins of the *Integral*. I see—the *Integral* is pondering its great, portentous future, the heavy load of unavoidable happiness it will carry upward, to you, unknown ones, who are forever searching and never finding. You shall find what you seek, you shall be happy—it is your duty to be happy, and you do not have much longer to wait.

The body of the *Integral* is almost ready: a graceful, elongated ellipsoid made of our glass—as eternal as gold, as flexible as steel. I saw the transverse ribs and the longitudinal stringers being attached to the body from within; in the stern they were installing the base for the giant rocket motor. Every three seconds, a blast; every three seconds the mighty tail of the *Integral* will eject flame and gases into cosmic space, and the fiery Tamerlane of happiness will soar away and away. . . .

I watched the men below move in regular, rapid rhythm, according to the Taylor system, bending, unbending, turning like the levers of a single huge machine. Tubes glittered in their hands; with fire they sliced and welded the glass walls, angles, ribs, brackets. I saw transparent glass monster cranes rolling slowly along glass rails, turning and bending as obediently as the men, delivering their loads into the bowels of the *Integral*. And all of this was one: humanized machines, perfect men. It was the highest, the most stirring beauty, harmony, music. . . . Quick! Below! To join them, to be with them!

And now, shoulder to shoulder, welded together with them, caught up in the steel rhythm . . . Measured movements; firmly round, ruddy cheeks; mirror-smooth brows, untroubled by the madness of thought. I floated on the mirror-smooth sea. I rested.

Suddenly one of them turned to me serenely. "Better today?"

"Better? What's better?"

"Well, you were out yesterday. We had thought

it might be something dangerous. ..." A bright forehead, a childlike, innocent smile.

The blood rushed to my face. I could not, could not lie to those eyes. I was silent, drowning. ...

The gleaming white round china face bent down through the hatch above. "Hey! D-503! Come up, please! We're getting a rigid frame here with the brackets, and the stress ..."

Without listening to the end, I rushed up to him. I was escaping ignominiously, in headlong flight. I could not raise my eyes. The glittering glass stairs flashed under my feet, and every step increased my hopelessness: I had no place here—I, the criminal, the poisoned one. Never again would I merge into the regular, precise, mechanical rhythm, never again float on the mirrorlike untroubled sea. I was doomed to burn forever, to toss about, to seek a corner where to hide my eyes—forever, until I finally found strength to enter that door and ...

And then an icy spark shot through me: I—well, I didn't matter; but I would also have to tell about her, and she, too, would be ...

I climbed out of the hatch and stopped on the deck. I did not know where to turn now, I didn't know why I had come there. I looked up. The midday-weary sun was rising dully. Below me was the *Integral*, gray-glassy, unalive. The rosy blood had trickled out. It was clear to me that all of this was merely my imagination, that everything remained as it had been before, yet it was also clear ...

"What's wrong with you, 503, are you deaf? I have been calling and calling. ... What's the matter?" The Second Builder shouted into my ear. He must have been shouting for a long time.

What's the matter with me? I have lost the rudder. The motor roars, the aero quivers and rushes at full speed, but there is no rudder, no controls, and I don't know where I'm flying: down—to crash into the ground in a moment, or up—into the sun, into the flames. ...

Sixteenth Entry

TOPICS: Yellow
Two-Dimensional Shadow
Incurable Soul

I have not written anything for several days, I don't know how many. All the days are one day. All the days are one color—yellow, like parched, fiery sand. And there is not a spot of shadow, not a drop of water. ... On and on endlessly over the yellow sand. I cannot live without her, yet since she vanished so incomprehensibly that day in the Ancient House, she ...

I have seen her only once since that day, during the daily walk. Two, three, four days ago—I do not know; all the days are one. She flashed by, filling for a second the yellow, empty world. And, hand in hand with her, up to her shoulder, the double-bent S and the paper-thin doctor. And there was a fourth one—I remember nothing but his fingers: they would fly out of the sleeves of his unif like clusters of rays, incredibly thin, white, long. I-330 raised her hand and waved to me. Over her neighbor's head she bent toward the one with the ray-like fingers. I caught the word *Integral*. All four glanced back at me. Then they were lost in the gray-blue sky, and again—the yellow, dessicated road.

That evening she had a pink coupon to visit me. I stood before the annunciator and implored it, with tenderness, with hatred, to click, to register in the white slot: I-330. Doors slammed; pale, tall, rosy, swarthy numbers came out of the elevator; shades were pulled down on all sides. She was not there. She did not come.

And possibly, just at this very moment, exactly at twenty-two, as I am writing this, she stands with closed eyes, leaning against someone with her shoulder, saying to someone, "Do you love?" To whom? Who is he? The one with the raylike fingers, or the thick-lipped, sputtering R? Or S?

S ... Why am I constantly hearing his flat steps all these days, splashing as through puddles? Why is he following me all these days like a shadow? Before me, beside me, behind—a gray-blue, two-dimensional shadow. Others pass through it, step on it, but it is invariably here, bound to me as by some invisible umbilical cord. Perhaps this cord is she—I-330? I don't know. Or perhaps they, the Guardians, already know that I ...

Suppose you were told: Your shadow sees you, sees you all the time. Do you understand me? And suddenly you have the strangest feeling: your hands are not your own, they interfere with you. And I catch myself constantly swinging my arms absurdly, out of time with my steps. Or suddenly I feel that I must glance back, but it's impossible, no matter how I try, my neck is rigid, locked. And I run, I run faster and faster, and feel with my back—my shadow runs faster behind me, and there is no escape, no escape anywhere. . . .

Alone, at last, in my room. But here there is something else—the telephone. I pick up the receiver. "Yes, I-330, please." And again I hear a rustle in the receiver, someone's steps in the hall, past her room—and silence. . . . I throw down the receiver—I can't, I can't endure it any longer. I must run there, to her.

This happened yesterday. I hurried there, and wandered for an hour, from sixteen to seventeen, near the house where she lives. Numbers marched past me, row after row. Thousands of feet stepped rhythmically, a million-footed monster floated, swaying, by. And only I was alone, cast out by a storm upon a desert island, seeking, seeking with my eyes among the gray-blue waves.

A moment, and I shall see the sharply mocking angle of the eyebrows lifted to the temples, the dark windows of the eyes, and there, within them, the burning fireplace, the stirring shadows. And I will step inside directly, I will say, "You know I cannot live without you. Why, then . . ." I will use the warm, familiar "thou"—only "thou."

But she is silent. Suddenly I hear the silence, I do not hear the Music Plant, and I realize it is past seventeen, everybody else is gone, I am alone, I am late. Around me—a glass desert, flooded by the yellow sun. In the smooth glass of the pavement, as in water, I see the gleaming walls suspended upside down, and myself, hung mockingly head down, feet up.

I must hurry, this very second, to the Medical Office to get a certificate of illness, otherwise they'll take me and . . . But perhaps that would be best? To stay here and calmly wait until they see me and take me to the Operational Section—and so put an end to everything, atone for everything at once.

A faint rustle, and a doubly bent shadow before me. Without looking, I felt two steel-gray gimlets drill into me. With a last effort, I smiled and said—I had to say something—"I . . . I must go to the Medical Office."

"What's the problem, then? Why do you stand here?"

Absurdly upside down, hung by the feet, I was silent, burning up with shame.

"Come with me," S said harshly.

I followed obediently, swinging my unnecessary, alien arms. It was impossible to raise my eyes; I walked all the way through a crazy, upside-down world: some strange machines, their bases up; people glued antipodally to the ceiling; and, lower still, beneath it all, the sky locked into the thick glass of the pavement. I remember: what I resented most of all was that, for this last time in my life, I was seeing everything in this absurdly upside-down, unreal state. But it was impossible to raise my eyes.

We stopped. A staircase rose before me. Another step, and I would see the figures in white medical smocks, the huge, mute Bell. . . .

With an enormous effort, I finally tore my eyes away from the glass underfoot, and suddenly the golden letters of MEDICAL OFFICE burst into my face. At that moment it had not even occurred to me to wonder why he had spared me, why he had brought me here instead of to the Operational Section. At a single bound I swung across the steps, slammed the door firmly behind me, and took a deep breath. I felt: I had not breathed since morning, my heart had not been beating—and it was only now that I had taken my first breath, only now that the sluices in my breast had opened. . . .

There were two of them: one short, with tubby legs, weighing the patients with his eyes as though lifting them on horns; the other paper-thin, with gleaming scissor-lips, his nose a finest blade. . . . The same one.

I rushed to him as to someone near and dear,

mumbling about insomnia, dreams, shadows, a yellow world. The scissor-lips gleamed, smiled.

"You're in a bad way! Apparently, you have developed a soul."

A soul? That strange, ancient, long-forgotten word. We sometimes use the words "soul-stirring," "soulless," but "soul" . . . ?

"Is it . . . very dangerous?" I muttered.

"Incurable," the scissors snapped.

"But . . . what, essentially, does it mean? I somehow don't . . . don't understand it."

"Well, you see . . . How can I explain it to you? . . . You are a mathematician, aren't you?"

"Yes."

"Well, then—take a plane, a surface—this mirror, say. And on this surface are you and I, you see? We squint against the sun. And here, the blue electric spark inside that tube, and there—the passing shadow of an aero. All of it only on the surface, only momentary. But imagine this impermeable substance softened by some fire; and nothing slides across it any more, everything enters into it, into this mirror world that we examined with such curiosity when we were children. Children are not so foolish, I assure you. The plane has acquired volume, it has become a body, a world, and everything is now inside the mirror—inside you: the sun, the blast of the whirling propeller, your trembling lips, and someone else's. Do you understand? The cold mirror reflects, throws back, but this one absorbs, and everything leaves its trace—forever. A moment, a faint line on someone's face—and it remains in you forever. Once you heard a drop fall in the silence, and you hear it now. . . ."

"Yes, yes, exactly. . . ." I seized his hand. I heard it now—drops falling slowly from the washstand faucet. And I knew: this was forever. "But why,

why suddenly a soul? I've never had one, and suddenly ... Why ... No one else has it, and I ... ?"

I clung even more violently to the thin hand; I was terrified of losing the lifeline.

"Why? Why don't you have feathers, or wings—only shoulder blades, the base for wings? Because wings are no longer necessary, we have the aero, wings would only interfere. Wings are for flying, and we have nowhere else to fly: we have arrived, we have found what we had been searching for. Isn't that so?"

I nodded in confusion. He looked at me with a scalpel-sharp laugh. The other heard it, pattered in from his office on his tubby feet, lifted my paper-thin doctor, lifted me on his horn-eyes.

"What's the trouble? A soul? A soul, you say? What the devil! We'll soon return to cholera if you go on that way. I told you" (raising the paper-thin one on his horns) "—I told you, we must cut out imagination. In everyone. . . . Extirpate imagination. Nothing but surgery, nothing but surgery will do. . . ."

He saddled his nose with huge X-ray glasses, circled around and around me for a long time, peered through the bones of my skull, examining the brain, and writing something in his book.

"Curious, most curious! Listen, would you consent to ... to being preserved in alcohol? It would be extremely useful to the One State. . . . It would help us prevent an epidemic. . . . Of course, unless you have some special reasons to ..."

"Well, you see," said the thin one, "Number D-503 is the Builder of the *Integral*, and I am sure it would interfere with ..."

"U-um." The other grunted and pattered back to his office.

We remained alone. The paper-thin hand fell lightly, gently on my hand, the profile face bent close to mine. He whispered, "I'll tell you in confidence—you are not the only one. It was not for nothing that my colleague spoke about an epidemic. Try to remember—haven't you noticed anything like it, very much like it, very similar in anyone else?" He peered at me closely. What was he hinting at? Whom did he mean? Could it be . . . ?

"Listen." I jumped up from the chair.

But he was already speaking loudly about other things. "As far as your insomnia and your dreams, I can suggest one thing—do more walking. Start tomorrow morning, go out and take a walk . . . well, let's say to the Ancient House."

He pierced me with his eyes again, smiling his thinnest smile. And it seemed to me—I saw quite clearly a word, a letter, a name, the only name, wrapped in the finest tissue of that smile. . . . Or was this only my imagination again?

I could barely wait until he wrote out a certificate of illness for that day and the next. Silently I pressed his hand once more, and ran out.

My heart, fast and light as an aero, swept me up and up. I knew—some joy awaited me tomorrow. What was it?

TOPICS: Through the Glass
I Am Dead
Corridors

I am completely bewildered. Yesterday, at the very moment when I thought that everything was already disentangled, that all the X's were found, new unknown quantities appeared in my equation.

The starting point of all the coordinates in this entire story is, of course, the Ancient House. It is the center of the axial lines of all the X's, Y's and Z's on which my whole world has been built of late. Along the line of X's (Fifty-ninth Avenue) I walked toward the starting point of the coordinates. All that had happened yesterday whirled like a hurricane within me: upside-down houses and people, tormentingly alien hands, gleaming scissors, sharp drops falling in the washstand—all this had happened, had happened once. And all of it, tearing my flesh, was whirling madly within, beneath the surface melted by a fire, where the "soul" was.

In order to carry out the doctor's prescription, I deliberately chose to walk along two lines at right angles instead of a hypotenuse. I was already on the second line—the road along the Green Wall. From the illimitable green ocean behind the Wall rose a wild wave of roots, flowers, branches, leaves. It reared, and in a moment it would roll and break and overwhelm me, and, instead of a man—the finest and most precise of instruments—I would be turned into . . .

But fortunately between me and the wild green ocean was the glass of the Wall. Oh, great, divinely bounding wisdom of walls and barriers! They are, perhaps, the greatest of man's inventions. Man ceased to be a wild animal only when he built the first wall. Man ceased to be a savage only when we had built the Green Wall, when we had isolated our perfect mechanical world from the irrational, hideous world of trees, birds, animals. . . .

Through the glass the blunt snout of some beast stared dully, mistily at me; yellow eyes, persistently repeating a single, incomprehensible thought. For a long time we stared into each other's eyes—those mine-wells from the surface world into another, subterranean one. And a question stirred within me: What if he, this yellow-eyed creature, in his disorderly, filthy mound of leaves, in his uncomputed life, is happier than we are?

I raised my hand, the yellow eyes blinked, backed away, and disappeared among the greenery. The paltry creature! What absurdity—that he could possibly be happier than we are! Happier than I, perhaps; but I am only an exception, I am sick.

But even I . . . The dark-red walls of the Ancient House were already before me, and the old woman's dear, ingrown mouth.

I rushed to her: "Is she here?"

The ingrown mouth opened slowly. "Which 'she'?"

"Oh, which, which! I-330, of course. . . . We came here together that day—by aero . . ."

"Oh, oh, I see. . . . I see. . . ."

The rays of wrinkles round the lips, sly rays from the yellow eyes, probing inside me, deeper and deeper. And at last, "Oh, well. . . . She's here, she came a little while ago."

She's here. I saw a shrub of silvery-bitter wormwood at the old woman's feet. (The courtyard of the Ancient House is part of the museum, carefully preserved in its prehistoric state.) A branch of the wormwood lay along the old woman's hand and she stroked it; a yellow strip of sunlight fell across her knees. And for an instant, I, the sun, the old woman, the wormwood, and the yellow eyes were one, bound firmly together by some invisible veins, and, pulsing through the veins, the same tumultuous, glorious blood. . . .

I am embarrassed to write about this now, but I have promised to be completely frank in these notes. Well, then: I bent and kissed the ingrown, soft, mossy mouth. The old woman wiped her lips and laughed.

I ran through the familiar, dim, echoing rooms—for some reason directly to the bedroom. And it was only at the door, when I had already seized the handle, that suddenly the thought came, What if she is not alone? I stopped and listened. But all I heard was the beating of my heart—not within, but somewhere near me.

I entered. The wide bed—smooth, untouched. The mirror. Another mirror in the closet door, and in the keyhole—the key with the antique ring. And no one.

I called quietly, "I-330! Are you here?" Then, still more quietly, with eyes closed, scarcely breathing, as though I were already on my knees before her, "Darling!"

Silence. Only the drops falling hurriedly into the washstand from the faucet. I cannot explain why, but at that moment it annoyed me. I turned the faucet firmly and went out. Clearly, she was not there. That meant she must be in some other "apartment."

I ran down the wide gloomy stairway, tried one door, another, a third. Locked. Everything was locked except "our" apartment—and that was empty. . . .

And yet, I turned back again without knowing why. I walked slowly, with difficulty; my shoes were suddenly as heavy as cast iron. I clearly remember thinking: It's a mistake to assume that the force of gravity is constant. Hence, all my formulas . . .

The thought broke off: a door slammed downstairs, someone's steps pattered quickly across the tiles. I—light again, lighter than light—rushed to the rail, to bend over, to say everything in one word, one cry—"You". . . .

I turned numb: below, etched against the dark square shadow of the window frame, swinging its rosy wing-ears, the head of S was hurrying across.

Lightning-fast, without reason (I still don't know the reason), I felt: He must not see me, he must not!

On tiptoe, pressing myself into the wall, I slipped upstairs, toward the unlocked apartment.

A moment at the door. His feet stamped dully up the stairs, he was coming here. If only the door . . . I pleaded with the door, but it was wooden, it creaked, squealed. I stormed past green, red, the yellow Buddha; I was before the mirrored door of the wardrobe: my face pale, listening eyes, lips . . . Through the tumult of blood, I heard the door creaking again. . . . It was he, he. . . .

I seized the key; the ring swayed. A flash of memory—again an instant thought, bare, unreasoning, a splinter of a thought: "That time I-330 ..." I quickly opened the closet door; inside, in the darkness, I shut it tightly. A step, and the ground rocked under my feet. Slowly, softly, I floated down somewhere, my eyes turned dark, I died.

Later, when I sat down to record these strange events, I searched my memory and looked up some books. Now, of course, I understand it: it was a state of temporary death, familiar to the ancients, but—as far as I know—entirely unknown among us.

I have no idea how long I was dead—perhaps no more than five or ten seconds. But after a time I revived and opened my eyes. It was dark, and I felt myself going down and down. . . . I stretched my hand and tried to grasp at something—it was scraped by a rough, rapidly moving wall. There was blood on my finger—clearly all this was not the product of my sick imagination. What was it, then?

I heard my broken, quivering breath (I am ashamed to confess this, but everything was so unexpected and incomprehensible). A minute, two, three—down and down. Finally, a soft thud; that which had been dropping under my feet was now motionless. In the dark I found a handle, pushed it; a door opened. Dim light. Behind me I saw a small square platform speeding up. I rushed to it—too late: I was trapped there—but where this "there" was I did not know.

A corridor. The silence weighed a thousand tons. Along the vaulted ceiling, lamps—an endless, shimmering, trembling line of dots. The place was a little like the "tubes" of our underground, but much narrower and made not of our glass but of some ancient material. A thought flashed through

96

my mind—the memory of the underground shelters where our ancestors supposedly hid during the Two Hundred Years' War. . . . No matter, I must go.

I must have walked some twenty minutes, then turned right. The corridor was wider here, the lamps brighter. A vague humming sound. Perhaps machines, perhaps voices, I could not tell, but I was near a heavy opaque door—the sound came from behind it.

I knocked. Then again, louder. The hum ceased. Something clanked, and the door swung open, heavily, slowly.

I don't know which of us was more astonished: before me stood my blade-sharp, paper-thin doctor. "You? Here?" And his scissor-lips snapped shut. And I—as though I had never known a single human word—I stared silently without comprehending what he was saying. He must have been telling me to leave, because he quickly pushed me with his flat paper stomach to the end of the brighter section of the corridor, then turned me around and gave me a shove from the back.

"But, sorry . . . I wanted . . . I thought that I-330 . . . But behind me . . ."

"Wait here," the doctor snapped, and vanished.

At last! At last she was near me, here—and what did it matter where this "here" was? The familiar, saffron-yellow silk, the bite-smile, the veiled eyes . . . My lips, hands, knees trembled; and in my head, the silliest thought: Vibration is sound. Trembling must make a sound. Then why isn't it audible?

Her eyes opened to me—all the way; I entered.

. . .

"I could not bear it any longer! Where have you been? Why?" I spoke quickly, incoherently, as in delirium, without tearing my eyes away from her. Or perhaps I merely thought this. "There was the shadow—following me. . . . I died—in the closet. . . . Because your . . . that one . . . he speaks with scissors. . . . I have a soul. . . . Incurable . . ."

"An incurable soul! My poor dear!" I-330 laughed—sprayed me with laughter, and the delirium was over, and drops of laughter rang, sparkled all around, and everything, everything was beautiful.

The doctor appeared again from around the corner—the marvelous, magnificent, thinnest doctor.

"Well." He stopped beside her.

"It's nothing, it's all right! I'll tell you later. A mere accident. . . . Tell them I shall return in . . . oh, fifteen minutes. . . ."

The doctor slipped away around the corner. She waited. The door closed with a dull thud. Then I-330 slowly, slowly pressed against me with her shoulder, arm, all of her, plunging a sharp sweet needle deeper and deeper into my heart, and we walked together, the two of us—one. . . .

I don't remember where we turned off into darkness, and in the darkness—up a flight of stairs, endlessly, silently. I could not see, but I knew: she walked just as I did, with closed eyes, blind, her head thrown back, her teeth biting her lips—and listened to the music, to my barely audible trembling.

I came to in one of the innumerable nooks in the yard of the Ancient House. A fence—bare, rocky ribs and yellow teeth of ruined walls. She opened her eyes and said, "The day after tomorrow, at sixteen." And she left.

Did all this really happen? I don't know. I will learn the day after tomorrow. There is only one real trace—the scraped skin on my right hand, on the tips of my fingers. But the Second Builder has assured me that he saw me touch the polishing wheel by accident with those fingers, and that is all there is to it. Well, it may be so. It may be. I don't know—I don't know anything.

TOPICS :   A Logical Jungle
            Wounds and Plaster
            Never Again

Yesterday I went to bed, and instantly sank into the very depths of sleep, like an overturned, overloaded ship. A heavy, dense mass of swaying green water. And then I slowly rose from the bottom, and somewhere in the middle depths I opened my eyes: my own room, morning, still green, congealed. A splinter of sunlight on the mirrored door of the closet, flashing into my eyes, preventing me from punctually fulfilling the hours of sleep prescribed by the Table of Hours. It would be best to open the closet door. But all of me seemed wrapped in cobwebs; the cobwebs even spread over my eyes; I had no strength to rise. ...

And yet I rose and opened—and suddenly, behind the mirrored door, struggling out of her dress, all rosy, I-330. By now I was so accustomed to the most incredible events, that, as I recall, I was not even surprised and asked no questions. I quickly stepped into the closet and breathlessly, blindly, greedily united with her. I can see it now: through the crack in the darkness, a sharp ray of sunlight

100

breaking like a flash of lightning on the floor, on the wall of the closet, rising higher ... and now the cruel, gleaming blade fell on the bare outstretched neck of I-330. ... And this was so terrifying that I could not bear it. I cried out, and opened my eyes again.

My room. Morning, still green, congealed. A splinter of sunlight on the closet door. Myself—in bed. A dream. But my heart still hammered madly, quivered, sprayed pain; aching fingers, knees. There was no doubt that all of it had happened. And I no longer knew what was dream and what reality. Irrational values were growing through everything solid, familiar, three-dimensional, and instead of firm, polished planes I was surrounded by gnarled, shaggy things. ...

It was still long before the bell. I lay thinking, and an extremely odd chain of logic unwound itself in my mind.

Every equation, every formula in the surface world has its corresponding curve or body. But for irrational formulas, for my $\sqrt{-1}$, we know of no corresponding bodies, we have never seen them. ... But the horror of it is that these invisible bodies exist, they must, they inevitably must exist: in mathematics, their fantastic, prickly shadows—irrational formulas—pass before us as on a screen. And neither mathematics nor death ever makes a mistake. So that, if we do not see these bodies in our world, there must be, there inevitably must be, a whole vast world for them—there, beyond the surface. ...

I jumped up without waiting for the bell and rapidly began to pace the room. My mathematics—until now the only firm and immutable island in my entire dislocated world—has also broken off its moorings, is also floating, whirling. Does it mean, then, that this preposterous "soul" is as real as my unif, as my boots, although I do not see them at the moment? (They are behind the mirrored closet door.) And if the boots are not a disease, why is the "soul" a disease?

I sought and could not find a way out of this wild thicket of logic. It was the same unknown and eerie jungle as that other one, behind the Green Wall, inhabited by the extraordinary, incomprehensible creatures that spoke without words. It seemed to me that I was seeing through thick glass something infinitely huge and at the same time infinitely small, scorpionlike, with a hidden yet constantly sensed sting—the $\sqrt{-1}$. . . . But perhaps this was nothing else but my "soul," which, like the legendary scorpion of the ancients, voluntarily stung itself with everything that . . .

The bell. It was day. All of this, without dying, without vanishing, was merely covered by the light of day, just as visible objects, without dying, are covered at night by the darkness. A vague, quivering mist filled my head. Through the mist I saw the long glass tables, the spherical heads chewing slowly, silently, in unison. From afar through the fog I heard the ticking of the metronome, and in time to this familiar, caressing music I mechanically counted to fifty along with everyone else: fifty prescribed chewing movements for each bite. And, mechanically, in time to the ticking, I descended and marked off my name in the book of departures—like everyone else. But I felt I lived apart from everyone, alone, behind a soft wall that muted outside sounds. And here, behind this wall—my world. . . .

But then, if this world is mine alone, why does it go into these notes? Why record all these absurd "dreams," closets, endless corridors? I am saddened to see that, instead of a harmonious and strict mathematical poem in honor of the One State, I am producing some sort of a fantastic adventure novel. Ah, if it were really nothing but a novel, and not my present life, filled with X's, $\sqrt{-1}$, and falls.

However, perhaps it is all for the best. You, my unknown readers, are most probably children compared to us, for we have been brought up by the One State and hence have reached the highest summits possible for man. And, like children, you will swallow without protest everything bitter I shall give you only when it is carefully coated with the thick syrup of adventure.

In the evening

Are you familiar with the feeling of speeding in an aero up and up the blue spiral, when the window is open and the wild wind whistles past your face? There is no earth, you forget the earth, it is as far from you as Saturn, Jupiter, Venus. This is how I live now. A storm-wind rushes at my face, and I have forgotten the earth, I have forgotten the sweet, rosy O. And yet the earth exists; sooner or later one must glide back to it, and I merely shut my eyes before the day for which her name—O-90— is entered in my Sexual Table.

This evening the distant earth reminded me of its existence.

Obeying the doctor's instructions (I sincerely, most sincerely want to get well), I wandered for two hours along the glass deserts of our precise, straight avenues. Everyone else was in the auditoriums, as prescribed by the Table of Hours, and only I was alone. . . . It was essentially an unnatural sight: imagine a human finger cut off from the whole, from the hand—a separate human finger, running, stooped and bobbing, up and down,

103

along the glass pavement. I was that finger. And the strangest, the most unnatural thing of all was that the finger had no desire whatever to be on the hand, to be with others. I wanted either to continue thus—by myself, or ... But why try to conceal it any longer—to be with her, with I-330, once again pouring all of myself into her through the shoulder, through the intertwined hands. ...

I returned home when the sun was already setting. The rosy ash of evening glowed on the glass walls, on the golden spire of the Accumulator Tower, in the voices and smiles of the numbers I met. How strange: the dying rays of the sun fall at exactly the same angle as those flaring in the morning, yet everything is altogether different. The rosiness is different: now it was quiet, just faintly tinged with bitterness, and in the morning it would again be seething, resonant.

Downstairs in the lobby, U, the controller, took a letter from under a pile of envelopes covered with the rosy ash and handed it to me. I repeat: she is a perfectly decent woman, and I am certain that her feelings toward me are most friendly. And yet, every time I see those sagging, gill-like cheeks, they somehow set my teeth on edge.

Holding out the letter with her gnarled hand, U sighed. But her sigh just barely ruffled the curtain that separated me from the world; my whole being was centered on the envelope that trembled in my hands—undoubtedly containing a letter from I-330.

A second sigh, heavily underscored by two lines, made me break away from the envelope. I looked up: between the gills through the bashful blinds of lowered eyelids—a sympathetic, enveloping, clinging smile. And then, "My poor, poor friend," with a sigh underscored by three lines and a barely noticeable nod at the letter, the contents of which she was, of course, in the line of duty, familiar with.

"No, really, I. . . . But why?"

"No, no, my dear, I know you better than you know yourself. I have long been watching you, and I can see that you need someone marching hand in hand with you through life who has been a student of life for many years. . . ."

I felt myself all plastered over by her cloying smile—the plaster that would cover the wounds about to be inflicted by the letter trembling in my hands. And finally, through the bashful blinds, almost whispering, "I shall think about it, my dear, I shall think about it. And be assured: if I feel myself strong enough . . . But no, I must first think about it. . . ."

Great Benefactor! Am I to . . . does she mean to say that . . .

There were spots before my eyes, thousands of sinusoids, and the letter jumped in my hand. I walked to the wall, nearer to the light. The sun was dying, and the dismal, dark rose ash fell, thickening steadily, upon me, the floor, my hands, the letter.

I tore the envelope, and quickly—the signature, the wound: it was not I-330, it was . . . O. And still another wound: a watery blot on the lower right-hand corner of the page—where the drop fell. . . . I detest blots, whatever the reason for them—ink, or . . . anything else. And I know that formerly I simply would have been annoyed, my eyes would have been offended by that annoying blot. Why, then, was this gray little spot now like a cloud, turning everything darker, more leaden? Or was this again my "soul"?

You know . . . or, perhaps, you do not know . . . I cannot say it properly, but it does not matter: now you know that without you there will be no day, no morning, no spring for me. Because R is to me only . . . but this is of no interest to you. At any rate, I am very grateful to him. Without him, alone, these past days, I don't know what I would have . . . During these days and nights I have lived ten or perhaps twenty years. And it seems to me that my room is not rectangular, but round and endless—around and around, and all is the same, and no doors anywhere.

I cannot live without you—because I love you. Because I see, I understand: today you don't need anyone, anyone in the world except her, the other one, and . . . you understand—just because I love you I must . . .

I need only two or three days to put together the pieces of me into some semblance of the former O-90, and then I will go and tell them myself that I withdraw my registration for you. And you must feel relieved, you must be happy. I shall never again . . . Farewell.

O.

Never again. Yes, it is better that way, she is right. But why, then, why . . .

Nineteenth Entry

In that strange corridor with the quivering line of dim lamps . . . or no, no, it was not there, it was later, when we were already in some hidden corner in the yard of the Ancient House . . . she said, "The day after tomorrow." That means today, and everything is winged. The day flies. Our *Integral* is ready for flight: the rocket motor has already been installed and was tested today on the ground. What magnificent, powerful blasts, and to me each of them was a salute in honor of her, the only, the unique one—in honor of today.

During the first firing a dozen or so numbers from the dock neglected to get out of the way—nothing remained of them except some crumbs and soot. I record with pride that this did not disturb the rhythm of our work for even a moment. No one recoiled; both we and our machines continued our straight-line and circular motions with the same precision as before, as though nothing had happened. Ten numbers are less than a hundred-millionth part of the population of the

One State; practically considered, it is an infinitesimal of the third order. Only the ancients were prone to arithmetically illiterate pity; to us it is ridiculous.

And it's ridiculous to me that yesterday I paid attention to a miserable little gray spot and even wrote about it in these pages. All of this is but that same "softening" of the surface which should be diamond-hard—as hard as our walls.

Sixteen o'clock. I did not go for my supplementary walk; who knows, she might take it into her head to come just now, when everything rings brightly with the sun. ...

I am almost alone in the house. Through the sun-drenched walls I can see far, both right and left and down, the empty rooms suspended in the air, repeating themselves as in a mirror. And only on the bluish stairway, faintly sketched in by the sun, a lean, gray shadow is sliding up. I hear the steps now—and I see through the door—I feel the plaster smile glued to me. Then past my door, and down another stairway. ...

The annunciator clicked. I threw myself to the narrow white slit, and ... and saw some unfamiliar male number (beginning with a consonant). The elevator hummed, the door slammed. Before me—a heavy brow, set carelessly, aslant, over the face. And the eyes ... a strange impression, as though his words were coming from under the scowling brow, where the eyes were.

"A letter for you from her," came from beneath the overhanging brow. "She asked that everything be done exactly as it says."

From under the jutting brow, the overhang, a glance around. There's no one, no one here; come, let me have it! With another glance around, he slipped me the envelope and left. I was alone.

No, not alone: in the envelope, the pink coupon, and the faintest fragrance—hers. It is she, she will come, she will come to me. Quickly the letter—to read it with my own eyes, to believe it all the way. . . .

But no, this cannot be true! I read again, skipping lines: "The coupon . . . and don't fail to lower the shades, as if I were really there. . . . It is essential that they think I . . . I'm very, very sorry. . . ."

I tore the letter to bits. In the mirror, for a second, my distorted, broken eyebrows. I took the coupon to tear it as I tore her note. . . .

"She asked that everything be done exactly as it says."

My hands slackened. The coupon dropped on the table. She is stronger than I. I'm afraid I will do what she asks. However . . . however, I don't know: we'll see, it's still a long time until evening. . . . The coupon lies on the table.

My tortured, broken eyebrows in the mirror. Why don't I have a doctor's note today as well? I would walk and walk endlessly, around the whole Green Wall, then drop into bed—to the very bottom. . . . But I must go to the thirteenth auditorium, I must wind all of myself up tightly to sit two hours—two hours—without stirring . . . when I need to scream and stamp my feet.

The lecture. How strange that the voice coming from the gleaming apparatus is not metallic, as usual, but somehow soft, furry, mossy. A woman's voice. I imagine her as she must have been once upon a time: tiny, a little bent hook of an old woman, like the one at the Ancient House.

The Ancient House . . . And everything bursts out like a fountain from below—and I must use all of my strength to steel myself again, or I will drown the auditorium with screams. Soft, furry words pass through me, and all that remains is the awareness that they have something to do with children, with child-breeding. I am like a photographic plate. I retain every impression with an oddly alien, indifferent, senseless precision: a golden crescent—the light reflected on the loud-speaker; under it, a child, a living illustration, stretches toward the crescent; the edge of its microscopic unif in its mouth; a tightly closed little fist, the little thumb inside it; a light shadow across the wrist—a plump, tiny fold. Like a photographic plate, I record: the bare foot hangs over the edge now, the rosy fan of toes is stepping on air—a moment, and it will tumble to the floor.

A woman's scream; a unif, spreading like transparent wings, flew up to the stage, caught the child; lips on the tiny fold across the wrist; she moved the child to the middle of the table, came down from the stage. Mechanically, my mind imprinted the rosy crescent of the lips, its horns down, blue saucer eyes filled to the brim. O. And, as if reading some harmonious formula, I suddenly realized the necessity, the logic of this trivial incident.

She sat down just behind me, on the left. I glanced back; she obediently took her eyes away from the table with the child; her eyes turned to me, entered me, and again: she, I, and the table on the stage—three points, and through these points—lines, projections of some inevitable, still unseen events.

I walked home along the green, twilit street, already gleaming with lights here and there. I heard all of myself ticking like a clock. And the hands of the clock would in a moment step across some figure—I would do something from which there would be no drawing back. She, I-330, needs someone to think she is with me. And I need her, and what do I care for her "need." I will not be a blind for someone else—I won't.

Behind me, familiar steps, as though splashing through puddles. I no longer glance back; I know—it is S. He'll follow me to the door, then he will probably stand below, on the sidewalk, his gimlets drilling up, into my room—until the shades fall, concealing someone's crime. . . .

He, my Guardian Angel, put a period to my thoughts. I decided—No, I won't. I decided.

When I came into my room and switched on the light, I did not believe my eyes: near the table stood O. Or, rather, hung, like an empty dress that had been taken off the body. It was as though not a single spring remained under her dress; her arms drooped, springless; her legs, her voice hung limply.

"I . . . about my letter. You received it? Yes? I must know the answer, I must—right now."

I shrugged. Gloating, as if she were to blame for everything, I looked at her brimming blue eyes and delayed to answer. Then, with enjoyment, stabbing her with every separate word, I said, "An answer? Well . . . You are right. Completely. About everything."

"Then . . ." (she tried to cover her trembling with a smile, but I saw it). "Very well! I'll go—I'll go at once."

She hung over the table. Lowered eyes, limp arms, legs. The crumpled pink coupon of the other one was still on the table. I quickly opened the manuscript of *We* and hid the coupon—more, perhaps, from myself than from O.

"You see, I'm still writing. Already 170 pages . . . It's turning into something so unexpected . . ."

A voice, a shadow of a voice: "Do you remember . . . on page seven . . . I let a drop fall, and you . . ."

Blue saucers—silent, hurried drops over the

111

brim, down the cheeks, and words, hurried, over the brim. "I can't, I will go in a moment. . . . I'll never again . . . let it be as you say. But I want, I must have your child—give me a child and I will go, I'll go!"

I saw all of her trembling under her unif, and I felt: in a moment, I too . . . I put my hands behind my back and smiled.

"You seem to be anxious for the Benefactor's Machine?"

And her words, like a stream over the dam: "It doesn't matter! But I will feel, I'll feel it within me. And then, if only for a few days . . . To see, to see just once the little crease, here—like that one, on the table. Only one day!"

Three points: she, I, and the tiny fist there, on the table, with the plump fold. . . .

Once, I remember, when I was a child, we were taken to the Accumulator Tower. On the very top landing, I bent over the glass parapet. Below, dots of people, and my heart thumped sweetly: What if? At that time I had merely seized the rail more firmly; now, I jumped.

"So you want it? Knowing that . . ."

Eyes closed, as if facing the sun. A wet, radiant smile. "Yes, yes! I do!"

I snatched the pink coupon from under the manuscript—the other's coupon—and ran downstairs, to the controller on duty. O caught my hand, cried out something, but I understood her words only when I returned.

She sat on the edge of the bed, her hands locked tightly between her knees. "That was . . . her coupon?"

"What does it matter? Well, yes, hers."

Something cracked. Or, perhaps, O merely stirred. She sat, hands locked in her knees, silently.

"Well? Hurry . . ." I roughly seized her hand,

and red spots (tomorrow they'll be blue) appeared on her wrist, by the plump childlike fold.

That was the last. Then—a click of the switch, all thought extinquished, darkness, sparks—I flew over the parapet, down. ...

TOPICS : Discharge
The Material of Ideas
Zero Crag

Discharge—this is the most fitting definition. Now I
see that it was precisely like an electrical discharge.
The pulse of my recent days had grown ever drier,
ever faster, ever more tense; the poles came ever
closer—a dry crackling—another millimeter: explosion, then—silence.

Everything in me is very quiet and empty now,
as in a house when everyone is gone and you are
lying alone, sick, and hearing with utmost clarity
the sharp, metallic ticking of your thoughts.

Perhaps this "discharge" has cured me finally of
my tormenting "soul," and I've become again like
all of us. At least, I can now visualize without any
pain O on the steps of the Cube; I can see her in
the Gas Bell. And if she names me there, in the
Operational Section, it does not matter: in my last
moment I shall piously and gratefully kiss the pun-
ishing hand of the Benefactor. Suffering punish-
ment is my right in relation to the One State, and
I will not yield this right. We, the numbers of our
State, should not, must not give up this right—the

only, and therefore the most precious, right that we possess.

My thoughts tick quietly, with metallic clarity. An unseen aero carries me off into the blue heights of my beloved abstractions. And there, in the purest, most rarefied air, I see my idea of "right" burst with the snap of a pneumatic tire. And I see clearly that it is merely a throwback to one of the absurd prejudices of the ancients—their notion of "rights."

There are clay ideas, and there are ideas forever carved of gold or of our precious glass. And, in order to determine the material of which an idea is made, it is enough to pour upon it a single drop of strong acid. One of these acids was known to the ancients too: *reductio ad finem*. I believe this is what they called it. But they were afraid of this poison, they preferred to see even a clay heaven, even a toy heaven, rather than blue nothing. But we, thanks to the Benefactor, are adults, we need no toys.

Well, then, suppose a drop of acid is applied to the idea of "rights." Even among the ancients, the most mature among them knew that the source of right is might, that right is a function of power. And so, we have the scales: on one side, a gram, on the other a ton; on one side "I," on the other "We," the One State. Is it not clear, then, that to assume that the "I" can have some "rights" in relation to the State is exactly like assuming that a gram can balance the scale against the ton? Hence, the division: rights to the ton, duties to the gram. And the natural path from nonentity to greatness is to forget that you are a gram and feel yourself instead a millionth of a ton.

You, pink-cheeked, full-bodied Venusians, and you, Uranians, sooty as blacksmiths, I hear your murmur of objections in my blue silence. But you must learn to understand: everything great is simple; only the four rules of arithmetic are eternal and immutable. And only an ethic built on the four rules can be great, immutable, and eternal. This is the ultimate wisdom, the summit of the pyramid, which people, flushed with perspiration, kicking and gasping, have been climbing for centuries. And from this summit, all that is below, in the depths, where the residual something surviving in us from our savage ancestors still stirs like a heap of miserable worms, is alike. From this summit all these are alike: the unlawful mother—O; the murderer; the madman who dared to fling his verses into the face of the One State. And the judgment meted out to them is alike: untimely death. This is that divine justice the stone-house people had dreamed of in the rosy, naïve light of the dawn of history. Their "God" punished blasphemy against the Holy Church as sternly as murder.

You, Uranians, as austere and dark as the ancient Spaniards who had the wisdom to burn offenders in blazing pyres, you are silent; I think you are on my side. But I hear the pink Venusians muttering something about torture, executions, a return to barbarian times. My dear friends, I pity you: you are incapable of philosophic-mathematical thought.

Human history ascends in circles, like an aero. The circles differ—some are golden, some bloody. But all are equally divided into three hundred and sixty degrees. And the movement is from zero—onward, to ten, twenty, two hundred, three hundred and sixty degrees—back to zero. Yes, we have returned to zero—yes. But to my mathematical mind it is clear that this zero is altogether different, altogether new. We started from zero to the right, we have returned to it from the left. Hence, instead of plus zero, we have minus zero. Do you understand?

I envisage this Zero as an enormous, silent, narrow, knife-sharp crag. In fierce, shaggy darkness, holding our breath, we set out from the black night side of Zero Crag. For ages we, the Columbuses, have sailed and sailed; we have circled the entire earth. And, at long last, hurrah! The burst of a salute, and everyone aloft the masts: before us is a different, hitherto unknown side of Zero Crag, illumined by the northern lights of the One State— a pale blue mass, sparks, rainbows, suns, hundreds of suns, billions of rainbows. . . .

What if we are but a knife's breadth away from the other, the black side of the crag? The knife is the strongest, the most immortal, the most brilliant of man's creations. The knife has been a guillotine; the knife is the universal means of solving all knots; along the knife's edge is the road of paradoxes—the only road worthy of a fearless mind.

Twenty-first Entry

TOPICS: An Author's Duty
The Ice Swells
The Most Difficult Love

Yesterday was her day, and once again she did not come, and once again she sent an inarticulate note, explaining nothing. But I am calm, I am completely calm. If nevertheless I follow the note's dictates, if I take down her coupon to the controller on duty and then, lowering the shades, sit in my room alone, it is not because I am unable to act against her wishes. Ridiculous! Of course not. It is simply because, protected by the shades from all the plaster-healing smiles, I can quietly write these pages. That is one. Second, I am afraid that if I lose I-330, I will also lose what is perhaps the only key to the disclosure of all the unknown quantities (the incident of the closet, my temporary death, and so on). And, even simply as the author of these notes, I feel that I am duty-bound to find the answers. Not to mention the fact that all unknowns are organically inimical to man, and *homo sapiens* is human in the full sense of the word only when his grammar is entirely free of question marks, when it has nothing but exclamation points, periods, and commas.

And so, guided, it seems to me, precisely by an author's obligation, I took an aero today at sixteen and proceeded once more to the Ancient House. I flew against a strong wind. The aero plowed with difficulty through the airy thickets, their invisible branches swishing and whipping at it. The city beneath me seemed built entirely of blue blocks of ice. Suddenly—a cloud, a swift slanting shadow, and the ice turned leaden, swelled as the ice on a river in springtime, when you are standing on the bank and waiting: a moment, and everything will burst, spill over, whirl, and rush downstream. But minutes pass, and the ice still holds; and you feel as though you yourself were swelling, and your heart beats faster, faster, with mounting disquiet. (But why am I writing all this, and whence these strange sensations? For there is surely no ice-breaker capable of crushing the most transparent, most enduring crystal of our life. . . .)

There was no one at the entrance to the Ancient House. I walked around it and found the old gatekeeper near the Green Wall. Her hand shielding her eyes, she was looking up. There, above the Wall—the sharp black triangles of some birds. Screaming, they dashed themselves against the firm, invisible barrier of electric waves, recoiled, and—back again over the Wall.

I saw their slanting shadows glide swiftly over her dark, wrinkled face, her swift glance at me.

"There's no one, no one here! No one! And no need to go in. No . . ."

What does she mean, no need? And what a strange notion—regarding me only as someone's shadow! What if all of them are only my shadows? Was it not I who populated with them all these pages—just recently no more than white rectangular deserts? Without me, would they ever be seen by those whom I shall lead behind me along the narrow paths of lines?

Naturally, I said nothing of all this to her. From my own experience I know that the cruelest thing is to make a person doubt his own reality, his three-dimensional—not any other—reality. I merely told her dryly that her job was to open the door, and she let me into the courtyard.

Empty. Quiet. Wind outside, behind the walls, distant as the day when, shoulder to shoulder, two as one, we came out from below, from the corridors —if, indeed, this ever really happened. I walked beneath stone archways where my steps, resounding from the damp vaults, seemed to fall behind me, as if someone followed on my heels. Yellow walls with scars of red brick watched me through the dark glass squares of their windows, watched me open the singing doors of barns, peer into corners, dead ends, nooks, and crannies. A gate in the fence, and a desolate vacant lot—memorial of the great Two Hundred Years' War. Rising from the earth— bare stony ribs, the yellow grinning jaws of walls, an ancient stove with a vertical chimney—a ship forever petrified among the stony splashes of red and yellow brick.

It seemed to me that I had seen those yellow teeth before, dimly, as through water, at the bottom of a deep lake. And I began to search. I stumbled into pits, tripped over rocks; rusty claws caught at my unif; sharp, salty drops of sweat crept down my forehead into my eyes. . . .

It was not there! I could not find it anywhere— that exit from below, from the corridors. It was not there. But then, it might be better this way: more likelihood that all of it had been one of my sense-less "dreams."

Exhausted, covered with dust and cobwebs, I

had already opened the gate to return to the main yard. Suddenly—a rustle behind me, splashing steps, and there, as I turned—the pink wing-ears, the double-curved smile of S.

Squinting, he bored through me with his gimlets, then asked, "Taking a stroll?"

I was silent. My hands were alien.

"Well, then, are you feeling better now?"

"Yes, thank you. I think I am returning to normal."

He released me—raised his eyes, threw back his head, and for the first time I noticed his Adam's apple.

Above us, at the height of no more than fifty meters, buzzed several aeros. By their low altitude, slow flight, and lowered black trunks of observation tubes, I recognized them: they were the aeros of the Guardians—not the usual group of two or three, but ten or twelve of them (unfortunately, I must confine myself to an approximate figure).

"Why are there so many today?" I ventured to ask.

"Why? Hm ... A true physician begins his cure with a healthy man, one who will get sick only tomorrow, or the day after tomorrow, or in a week. Prophylaxis, you see!"

He nodded, and plashed away across the stone slabs of the yard. Then he turned, and over his shoulder, "Be careful!"

I was alone. Quiet. Empty. Far above the Green Wall the wind, the birds were tossing about. What did he mean?

My aero glided swiftly down the current. Light, heavy shadows of clouds; below—blue cupolas, cubes of glass ice turned leaden, swollen . . .

I opened my manuscript to jot down in these pages some thoughts that I believe will prove useful (to you, my readers), thoughts about the great Day of Unanimity, which is approaching. And then I realized I could not write tonight. I was listening constantly to the wind as it flapped its dark wings against the window; I was constantly turning back, waiting. For what? I did not know. And when the familiar brownish-pink gills appeared in my room, I confess I was glad. She sat down, modestly smoothed out the fold of her unif which fell between her knees, quickly plastered me all over with her smiles, a piece on every crack—and I felt myself pleasantly, firmly bound.

"You know, I came to class today (she works at the Child-Rearing Factory) and found a caricature on the wall. Yes, yes, I assure you! They drew me as a kind of fish. Perhaps I am really . . ."

"Oh, no, no, of course not," I hastened to say. (From nearby, there was really nothing in her face resembling gills, and my words about gills had been entirely wrong.)

"Well, anyway, that isn't important. But, you understand, the act itself. Naturally, I called out the Guardians. I am very fond of children, and I believe that the most difficult and noble love is— cruelty. Do you understand it?"

I certainly did! It echoed my own thoughts. I could not refrain from reading to her a fragment from my Twentieth Entry, beginning with "My thoughts tick quietly, with metallic clarity."

Without looking up, I saw the quivering of her brown-pink cheeks, drawing closer and closer to me, and now her dry, hard, almost pricking fingers were on my hands.

"Give it to me, give it to me! I will record it and have the children memorize it. We need this more than your Venusians, we need it—today, tomorrow, the day after tomorrow."

She glanced over her shoulder and almost whispered, "Have you heard? They say that on the Day of Unanimity ..."

I jumped up. "What—what do they say? What about the Day of Unanimity?"

The comfortable walls had disappeared. I instantly felt myself flung out, there, where the immense wind tossed over the roofs and the slanting twilit clouds sank lower and lower. ...

U resolutely, firmly grasped my shoulders, although I noticed that, as if resonating to my own agitation, her bony fingers trembled.

"Sit down, my dear, don't get upset. People say all sorts of things, it doesn't matter. And then—if only you need it, I shall be with you on that day. I'll leave my children with someone else and be with you; for you, my dear, are also a child, and you need ..."

"No, no." I waved her away. "Certainly not! Then you will really think that I am a child, that I cannot ... by myself ... Certainly not!" (I must confess that I had other plans for that day.)

She smiled. The unspoken meaning of the smile was obviously, "Ah, what an obstinate boy!" She sat down, eyes lowered, hands modestly straightening again the fold of her unif that dropped between her knees. And then she turned to something else. "I think I must decide . . . for your sake . . . No, I beg you, don't hurry me, I must still think about it. . . ."

I did not hurry her, although I realized that I ought to be pleased, and that there was no greater honor than gracing someone's evening years.

All that night I was tormented by wings. I walked about shielding my head with my hands from the wings. And then, there was the chair. Not one of ours, not a modern glass chair, but an ancient wooden one. It moved like a horse—front right foot, rear left, front left, rear right. It ran up to my bed, climbed into it, and I made love to the wooden chair. It was uncomfortable and painful.

Amazing: can't anyone invent a remedy for this dream-sickness? Or else turn it into something rational, or even useful?

Twenty-second Entry

TOPICS : Congealed Waves
Everything Is Being Perfected
I Am a Microbe

Imagine yourself standing on the shore: the waves rise rhythmically, then, having risen, suddenly remain there—frozen, congealed. It seemed just as eerie and unnatural when our daily walk, prescribed by the Table of Hours, suddenly halted midway, and everyone was thrown into confusion. The last time something similar happened, according to our annals, was 119 years ago, when a meteorite dropped, smoking and whistling, right into the thick of the marching rows.

We walked as usual, in the manner of the warriors on Assyrian reliefs: a thousand heads, two fused, integral feet, two integral, swinging arms. At the end of the avenue, where the Accumulator Tower hummed sternly, a rectangle moved toward us. In front, behind, and on the sides—guards; in the middle—three people, the golden numbers already removed from their unifs. And everything was terrifyingly clear.

The huge clock atop the Tower was a face; leaning from the clouds, spitting down seconds, it

125

waited indifferently. And then, exactly at six minutes past thirteen, something went wrong in the rectangle. It happened quite near me, and I saw every detail; I clearly remember the thin long neck and the network of blue veins on the temple, like rivers on the map of some tiny unknown world, and this unknown world was evidently a very young man. He must have noticed someone in our ranks; rising to his toes, he stretched his neck, and stopped. A click: one of the guards sent the blue spark of an electric whip across him, and he squealed thinly, like a puppy. Then—a series of distinct clicks, about every two seconds: a click, and a squeal, a click, and a squeal.

We continued our rhythmic, Assyrian walk, and, looking at the graceful zigzags of the sparks, I thought: Everything in human society is being continually perfected—and should be. What a hideous weapon was the ancient whip—and how beautiful . . .

But at this moment, like a nut slipping off a machine in full swing, a slender, pliant female figure broke from our ranks and with the cry "Enough! Don't dare to . . . !" she threw herself into the midst of the rectangle. It was like that meteor, 119 years ago: the whole procession stopped dead, and our ranks were like the gray crests of waves congealed by a sudden frost.

For a moment I looked at her as a stranger, like everyone else. She was no longer a number—she was only a human being, she existed only as the metaphysical substance of an insult thrown in the face of the One State. But then one of her movements—turning, she swung her hips to the left—and all at once I felt: I know, I know this body, pliant as a whip! My eyes, my lips, my arms know it! At that moment I was completely certain of it.

Two of the guards stepped out to intercept her.

In a second, their trajectories will cross over that still limpid, mirrorlike point of the pavement—in a moment she will be seized. . . . My heart gulped, stopped, and without reasoning—is it allowed, forbidden, rational, absurd?—I flung myself toward that point.

I sensed upon me thousands of terrified, wide-open eyes, but this merely fed the desperate, gay, exulting strength of the hairy-armed savage who broke out of me, and he ran still faster. Only two steps remained. She turned. . . .

Before me was a trembling, freckled face, red eyebrows. . . . It was not she, not I-330.

Wild burst of joy. I wanted to cry out something like "Right, hold her!" but I heard only a whisper. And on my shoulder—a heavy hand. I was held, I was being taken somewhere, I tried to explain to them. . . .

"But listen, but you must understand, I thought that . . ."

But how explain all of myself, all of my sickness, recorded in these pages? And I subsided and walked obediently. . . . A leaf torn off a tree by a sudden blast of wind obediently falls downward, but on the way it whirls, catches at every familiar branch, fork, knot. And I, too, was catching at every silent spherical head, at the transparent ice of the walls, at the blue spire of the Accumulator Tower piercing a cloud.

At that moment, when an impenetrable curtain was just about to cut me off from this whole, beautiful world, I saw nearby, swinging his pink earwings, gliding over the mirror-smooth pavement, a huge, familiar head. And a familiar, flattened voice: "It is my duty to inform you that Number D-503 is ill and incapable of controlling his emotions. And I am sure that he was carried away by natural indignation. . . ."

"Yes, yes." I seized at it. "I even cried 'Hold her!'"

Behind my back: "You did not cry anything."

"Yes, but I wanted to—I swear by the Benefactor, I did."

For a second the gray, cold gimlet-eyes drilled through me. I don't know whether he saw within me that this was (almost) the truth, or whether he had some secret purpose of his own in sparing me again for a while, but he wrote out a note and gave it to one of those who held me. And I was free again, or, to be more exact, was returned again to the regular, endless Assyrian ranks.

The rectangle, containing both the freckled face and the temple with the map of bluish veins, disappeared around the corner, forever. We walked—a single million-headed body, and within each of us—that humble joy which probably fills the lives of molecules, atoms, phagocytes. In the ancient world this was understood by the Christians, our only predecessors (however imperfect): humility is a virtue, and pride a vice; "We" is from God, and "I" from the devil.

And now I was marching in step with everyone—yet separated from them. I still trembled from the recent excitement, like a bridge after an ancient iron train rushed, clattering, across it. I felt myself. But only an eye with a speck of dust in it, an abscessed finger, an infected tooth feel themselves, are aware of their individuality; a healthy eye, finger, tooth are not felt—they seem nonexistent. Is it not clear that individual consciousness is merely a sickness?

Perhaps I am no longer a phagocyte, busily and calmly devouring microbes (with bluish temples and freckles). Perhaps I am a microbe, and perhaps there are already thousands of them among us, still—like myself—pretending to be phagocytes.

. . .

What if today's essentially unimportant incident
... what if it is only a beginning, only the first
meteorite of a hail of thundering fiery rocks
poured by infinity upon our glass paradise?

TOPICS: Flowers
The Dissolution of a Crystal
If Only

It is said there are flowers that bloom only once in a hundred years. Why should there not be some that bloom once in a thousand, in ten thousand years? Perhaps we never knew about them simply because this "once in a thousand years" has come only today?

Blissfully, drunkenly, I walked down the stairs to the number on duty, and all around me, wherever my eyes fell, thousand-year-old buds were bursting into bloom. Everything bloomed—armchairs, shoes, golden badges, electric bulbs, someone's dark, shaggy eyes, the faceted columns of the banisters, a handkerchief someone dropped on the stairs, the table of the number on duty, and the delicately brown, speckled cheeks of U over the table. Everything was extraordinary, new, delicate, rosy, moist.

U took the pink coupon, and above her head, through the glass wall, the moon, pale blue, fragrant, swayed from an unseen branch. I pointed triumphantly at the moon and said, "The moon—you understand?"

U glanced at me, then at the number on the coupon, and I saw again that enchantingly modest, familiar movement of her hand, smoothing the folds of the unif between the angles of her knees.

"My dear, you don't look normal, you look sick—for abnormality and sickness are the same thing. You are ruining yourself, but no one, no one will tell you that."

That "no one" is, of course, equated with the number on the coupon: I-330. Dear, marvelous U! Of course you are right: I am imprudent, I am sick, I have a soul, I am a microbe. But isn't blooming a sickness? Doesn't it hurt when a bud splits open? And don't you think that spermatozoa are the most terrible of microbes?

Back upstairs, in my room. In the wide-open calyx of the chair—I-330. I am on the floor, embracing her legs, my head in her lap. We do not speak. Silence, heartbeats . . . And I am a crystal, I dissolve in her. I feel with utmost clarity how the polished facets that delimit me in space are melting away, away—I vanish, dissolve in her lap, within her, I grow smaller and smaller and at the same time ever wider, ever larger, expanding into immensity. Because she is not she, but the universe. And for a moment I and this chair near the bed, suffused with joy, are one. And the magnificently smiling old woman at the gate of the Ancient House, and the wild jungle beyond the Green Wall, and some silver ruins on black ground, dozing like the old woman, and the slamming of a door somewhere, immeasurably far away—all this is in me, with me, listening to the beating of my pulse and rushing through the blessed second. . . .

In absurd, confused, flooded words I try to tell her that I am a crystal, and therefore there is a door in me, and therefore I feel the happiness of the chair she sits in. But the words are so nonsensical that I stop, ashamed: I—and suddenly such ...

"Darling, forgive me! I don't know—I talk such nonsense, so foolishly. ..."

"And why do you think that foolishness is bad? If human foolishness had been as carefully nurtured and cultivated as intelligence has been for centuries, perhaps it would have turned into something extremely precious."

"Yes. ..." (It seems to me that she is right—how could she be wrong at this moment?)

"And for one foolish action—for what you did the other day during the walk—I love you still more, much more."

"But why did you torment me, why didn't you come, why did you send me your coupons and make me ..."

"Perhaps I had to test you? Perhaps I must know that you will do whatever I wish—that you are altogether mine?"

"Yes, altogether!"

She took my face—all of me—in her hands and raised my head. "And what about your 'duty of every honest number'? Eh?"

Sweet, sharp, white teeth; a smile. In the open calyx of the chair she is like a bee—a sting, and honey.

Yes, duties ... Mentally I turn the pages of my latest entries: not a hint of a thought anywhere that, actually, I should ...

I am silent. I smile ecstatically (and probably foolishly), look into her pupils, run with my eyes from one to the other, and in each of them I see myself: I, tiny, infinitesimal, am caught in these tiny rainbow prisons. And then again—bees—lips, the sweet pain of blooming ...

In every number there is an invisible, quietly ticking metronome, and we know the time exactly to within five minutes without looking at a clock. But now my metronome had stopped, I did not know how much time had passed. Anxiously, I drew out the badge with my watch from under the pillow.

Thanks to the Benefactor! We still have twenty minutes. But minutes, so ridiculously short, are running fast, and I must tell her so much—everything, all of me: about O's letter, about that dreadful evening when I gave her a child; and also, for some reason, about my childhood—about the mathematician Plapa, about $\sqrt{-1}$, about my first time at the Day of Unanimity, when I cried bitterly because, on such a day, there turned out to be an inkspot on my unif.

I-330 raised her head, leaned on her elbow. At the corners of her lips, two long, sharp lines, and the dark angle of raised eyebrows: a cross.

"Perhaps, on that day ..." She broke off, her brow darkening. She took my hand and pressed it hard. "Tell me, you will not forget me, you will remember me always?"

"Why do you speak like that? What do you mean? My darling!"

She was silent, and her eyes now looked past me, through me, far away. I suddenly heard the wind flapping huge wings against the glass (of course, this had gone on all the time, but I had not heard it until now), and for some reason I recalled the piercing birds over the top of the Green Wall.

She shook her head, as if to free herself of something. Again, for a second, she touched me with all of herself—as an aero touches the earth for a moment, springlike, before settling down.

"Well, give me my stockings now! Hurry!"

Her stockings, thrown on the table, rested on the open page of my manuscript (the 193rd). In my haste, I swept off the manuscript, the pages scattered, I would never be able to collect them in order again. And even if I did, there would be no real order; some gaps, some obstacles, some X's would remain.

"I can't go on this way," I said. "You are here, next to me, and yet you seem to be behind an ancient, opaque wall. I hear a rustling, voices behind the wall, but cannot make out the words; I don't know what is there. I cannot bear it. You are forever keeping something back, you've never told me where I was that time in the Ancient House, and what those corridors were, and why the doctor. Or, perhaps, this never really happened?"

I-330 put her hands on my shoulders, and slowly entered deep into my eyes. "You want to know everything?"

"Yes, I want to. I must."

"And you won't be afraid to follow me anywhere, to the very end—wherever I might lead you?"

"Anywhere!"

"Good. I promise you: after the holiday, if only ... Oh, by the way, how is your *Integral* doing? I always forget to ask—how soon?"

"No, what do you mean, 'if only'? Again? 'If only' what?"

But she, already at the door: "You'll see yourself. . . ."

I am alone. All that remains of her is a faint fragrance, reminiscent of the sweet, dry, yellow pollen of some flowers from behind the Wall. And also—the little hooks of questions firmly stuck within me—like those used by the ancients in catching fish (Prehistoric Museum).

Why did she suddenly think of the *Integral*?

I am like a machine set at excessive speed: the
bearings are overheated; another minute, and molten metal will begin to drip, and everything will
turn to naught. Quick—cold water, logic. I pour it
by the pailful, but logic hisses on the red-hot bearings and dissipates into the air in whiffs of white,
elusive steam.

Of course, it's clear: in order to determine the
true value of a function it is necessary to take it to
its ultimate limit. And it is clear that yesterday's
preposterous "dissolution in the universe," brought
to its ultimate point, means death. For death is
precisely the most complete dissolution of self in
the universe. Hence, if we designate love as "L"
and death as "D," then $L = f(D)$. In other
words, love and death . . .

Yes, exactly, exactly. This is why I am afraid of
I-330, I resist her, I don't want to . . . But why
does this "I don't want" exist within me together
with "I want"? That's the full horror of it—I long
for last night's blissful death again. That's the

135

horror of it, that even today, when the logical function has been integrated, when it is obvious that death is implicit in this function, I still desire her, with my lips, arms, breast, with every millimeter of me. ...

Tomorrow is Unanimity Day. She will, of course, be there too, I'll see her, but only from a distance. From a distance—that will be painful, because I must, I am irresistibly drawn to be near her, so that her hands, her shoulder, her hair ... But I long even for this pain—let it come.

Great Benefactor! How absurd—to long for pain. Who doesn't know that pain is a negative value, and that the sum of pain diminishes the sum we call happiness? And hence ...

And yet—there is no "hence." Everything is blank. Bare.

In the evening

Through the glass walls of the house—a windy, feverishly pink, disquieting sunset. I turn my chair away from that intruding pinkness and turn the pages of my notes. And I can see: again I have forgotten that I am writing not for myself, but for you, unknown readers, whom I love and pity—for you who are still trudging somewhere below, behind, in distant centuries.

Well, then—about Unanimity Day, this great holiday. I have always loved it, since childhood. It seems to me that to us it has a meaning similar to that of "Easter" to the ancients. I remember, on the eve of this day I would prepare for myself a sort of hour calendar—then happily cross out each hour: an hour nearer, an hour less to wait. ... If I were certain that nobody would see it, honestly, I would carry such a little calendar with me even today, watching by it how many hours remain until tomorrow, when I will see—if only from a distance ...

(I was interrupted: they brought me a new unif, fresh from the factory. We usually receive new unifs for this day. In the hallway outside—steps, joyful exclamations, noise.)

I continue. Tomorrow I will see the spectacle which is repeated year in, year out, and yet is ever new, and ever freshly stirring: the mighty chalice of harmony, the reverently upraised arms. Tomorrow is the day of the annual elections of the Benefactor. Tomorrow we shall again place in the Benefactor's hands the keys to the imperishable fortress of our happiness.

Naturally, this is entirely unlike the disorderly, disorganized elections of the ancients, when—absurd to say—the very results of the elections were unknown beforehand. Building a state on entirely unpredictable eventualities, blindly—what can be more senseless? And yet apparently it needed centuries before man understood this.

Needless to say, among us, in this respect as in all others, there is no room for eventualities; nothing unexpected can occur. And the elections themselves are mainly symbolic, meant to remind us that we are a single, mighty, million-celled organism, that—in the words of the ancients—we are the Church, one and indivisible. Because the history of the One State knows of no occasion when even a single voice dared to violate the majestic unison.

It is said that the ancients conducted their elections in some secret manner, concealing themselves like thieves. Some of our historians even assert that they came to the election ceremonies carefully masked. (I can imagine that fantastically gloomy sight: night, a square, figures in dark cloaks moving stealthily along the walls; the scarlet flame of torches flattened by the wind. ...) No one has yet discovered the full reason for all this secrecy; it is most likely that elections were connected with some mystical, superstitious, or even criminal rites. But we have nothing to conceal or be ashamed of; we celebrate elections openly, honestly, in broad daylight. I see everyone voting for the Benefactor; everyone sees me voting for the Benefactor. And, indeed, how could this be otherwise, since "everyone" and "I" are a single "We." How infinitely more ennobling, sincere, and lofty this is than the cowardly, stealthy "secrecy" of the ancients! And also—how much more expedient. For even assuming the impossible—some dissonance in the usual monophony—the unseen Guardians are right there, in our ranks. They can immediately take note of the numbers of those who have strayed and save them from further false steps—thus saving the One State from them. And, finally, one more ...

Through the wall on the left—a woman hastily unfastening her unif before the glass door of the closet. And for a second, a glimpse of eyes, lips, two sharp rosy points. ... Then the blind falls, and all that happened yesterday is instantly upon me, and I no longer know what "finally, one more" was meant to be, I want to know nothing about it, nothing! I want one thing—I-330. I want her with me every minute, any minute, always—only with me. And all that I have just written about Unanimity is unnecessary, entirely beside the point, I want to cross it out, tear it up, throw it away. Because I know (this may be blasphemy, but it is true), the only holiday for me is to be with her, to have her near me, shoulder to shoulder. And without her, tomorrow's sun will be nothing but a small circle cut of tin, and the sky, tin painted blue, and I myself ...

I snatch the telephone receiver. "I-330, is it you?"

"Yes, I. You're calling so late."

"Perhaps it is not too late. I want to ask you ... I want you to be with me tomorrow. Darling ..."

I said the last word almost in a whisper. And for some reason, the memory of an incident this morning at the building site flashed before me. In jest, someone had placed a watch under a hundred-ton hammer—the hammer swung, a gust of wind in the face, and a hundred tons delicately, quietly came to rest upon the fragile watch.

A pause. It seems to me that I hear someone's whisper there, in her room. Then her voice: "No, I cannot. You understand—I would myself ... No, no, I cannot. Why? You will see tomorrow."

Night

Twenty-fifth Entry

TOPICS: Descent from Heaven
The Greatest Catastrophe in
History
The Known Is Ended

Before the ceremony, everyone stood still and, like a solemn, slow canopy, the Hymn swayed over our heads—hundreds of trumpets from the Music Plant and millions of human voices—and for a second I forgot everything. I forgot the disquieting hints of I-330 about today's celebration; I think I forgot even her. I was the boy who had once wept on this day over a tiny spot on his unif, visible to no one but himself. No one around may see the black, indelible spots I am covered with, but I know that I—a criminal—have no right to be among these frank, wide-open faces. If I could only stand up and shout, scream out everything about myself. And let it mean the end—let it!—if only for a moment I can feel myself as pure and thoughtless as this childishly innocent blue sky.

All eyes were raised. In the unblemished morning blue, still moist with night's tears—a barely visible speck, now dark, now glowing in the sun's rays. It was He, the new Jehovah, coming down to us from heaven, as wise and loving-cruel as the

Jehovah of the ancients. He came nearer and nearer, and millions of hearts rose higher and higher to meet Him. Now He sees us. And, together with Him, I mentally look down from above on the concentric circles of the platforms, marked by the thin blue dotted lines of our unifs, like cobweb circles spangled with microscopic suns (our gleaming badges). And in a moment, He will sit down in the center of the cobweb, the white wise Spider— the white-robed Benefactor, who has wisely bound us hand and foot with the beneficent nets of happiness.

But now His majestic descent from heaven was completed, the brass tones of the Hymn were silent, everyone sat down—and instantly I knew: all of this was indeed the finest cobweb; it was stretched tautly, it quivered—in a moment it would break and something unthinkable would happen . . .

Rising slightly in my seat, I glanced around, and my eyes met lovingly anxious eyes running from face to face. Now one number raised his hand, and, with a scarcely noticeable movement of his fingers, he signaled to another. And then—an answering signal. And another. . . . I understood: these were the Guardians. I knew they were alarmed by something; the cobweb, stretched, was quivering. And within me—as in a radio receiver set on the same wave length—there was an answering quiver.

On the stage, a poet read a pre-election ode, but I did not hear a single word—only the measured swaying of a hexametric pendulum, and every movement brought nearer some unknown appointed hour. I was still feverishly scanning the rows— face after face, like pages—and still failing to find the only one, the one I sought, I had to find it, quickly, for in a moment the pendulum would tick, and then . . .

He, it was he, of course. Below, past the stage, the rosy wing-ears slid past over the gleaming glass, the running body reflected as a dark, doubly curved S. He hurried somewhere in the tangled passages among the platforms.

S, I-330—there is some thread that links them (all the time I've sensed this thread between them; I still don't know what it is; some day I'll disentangle it). I fastened my eyes on him; like a ball of cotton he rolled farther and farther, the thread trailing behind him. Now he stopped, now ...

Like a lightning-quick, high-voltage discharge: I was pierced, twisted into a knot. In my row, at no more than forty degrees from me, S stopped, bent down. I saw I-330, and next to her—the revoltingly thick-lipped, grinning R-13.

My first impulse was to rush there and cry out, "Why are you with him today? Why didn't you want me to ...?" But the invisible, beneficent cobweb tightly bound my hands and feet; with teeth clenched, I sat as stiff as iron, my eyes fixed on them. As now, I remember the sharp physical pain in my heart. I thought: If nonphysical causes can produce physical pain, then it is clear that ...

Unfortunately, I did not bring this to conclusion. I recall only that something flashed about a "soul," and then the absurd ancient saying, "His heart dropped into his boots." And I grew numb. The hexameters were silent. Now it will begin. ... But what?

The customary five-minute pre-election recess. The customary pre-election silence. But now it was not the usual prayerlike, worshipful silence: now it was as with the ancients, when our Accumulator Towers were still unknown, when the untamed sky had raged from time to time with "storms." This silence was the silence of the ancients before a storm.

The air—transparent cast iron. It seemed one had to open the mouth wide to breathe. The ear, tense to the point of pain, recorded, somewhere behind, anxious whispers, like gnawing mice. With lowered eyes, I saw before me all the time those two, I-330 and R, side by side, shoulder to shoulder—and on my knees, my hateful, alien, shaggy, trembling hands. . . .

In everyone's hand, the badge with the watch. One. Two. Three . . . Five minutes . . . From the stage—the slow, cast-iron voice: "Those in favor will raise their hands."

If only I could look into His eyes as in the past—directly and devotedly: "Here I am, all of me. Take me!" But now I did not dare. With a great effort, as though all my joints were rusty, I raised my hand.

The rustle of millions of hands. Someone's stifled "Ah!" And I felt that something had already begun, was dropping headlong, but I did not know what, and did not have the strength—did not dare— to look. . . .

"Who is against?"

This always has been the most solemn moment of the ceremony: everyone continued sitting motionless, joyously bowing his head to the beneficent yoke of the Number of Numbers. But this time, with horror, I heard a rustling again, light as a sigh—more audible than the brass trumpets of the Hymn. Thus a man will sigh faintly for the last time in his life and all the faces around him turn pale, with cold drops on their foreheads.

I raised my eyes, and . . .

It took one-hundredth of a second: I saw thousands of hands swing up—"against"—and drop. I saw the pale, cross-marked face of I-330, her raised hand. Darkness fell on my eyes.

Another hair's breadth. A pause. Silence. My

pulse. Then, all at once, as at a signal from some mad conductor, shouts, crashing on all the platforms, the whirl of unifs swept in flight, the figures of the Guardians rushing about helplessly, someone's heels in the air before my eyes, and near them someone's mouth wide open in a desperate, unheard scream. For some reason, this etched itself in memory more sharply than anything else: thousands of silently screaming mouths, as on some monstrous movie screen.

And just as on a screen—somewhere far below, for a second—O's whitened lips. Pressed to the wall of a passage, she stood shielding her stomach with crossed arms. Then she was gone, swept away, or I forgot her because ...

This was no longer on a screen—it was within me, in my constricted heart, in my hammering temples. Over my head on the left, R-13 jumped suddenly up on the bench—spluttering, red, frenzied. In his arms—I-330, her unif torn from shoulder to breast, red blood on white. ... She held him firmly around the neck, and he, repulsive and agile as a gorilla, was carrying her up, away, bounding in huge leaps from bench to bench.

As during a fire in ancient days, everything turned red before me, and only one impulse remained—to jump, to overtake them. I cannot explain to myself where I found such strength, but, like a battering ram, I tore through the crowd, stepping on shoulders, benches—and now I was upon them; I seized R by the collar: "Don't you dare! Don't you dare, I say. Let her go. This very moment!" (My voice was inaudible—everyone shouted, everyone ran.)

"Who? What is it? What?" R turned, his sputtering lips shaking. He must have thought he had been seized by one of the Guardians.

144

"What? I won't have it, I won't allow it! Put her down—at once!"

He merely slapped his lips shut in anger, tossed his head, and ran on. And at this point—I am terribly ashamed to write about it, but I feel I must, I must record it, so that you, my unknown readers, may learn the story of my sickness to the very end—at this point I swung at his head. You understand—I struck him! I clearly remember this. And I remember, too, the feeling of release, the lightness that spread throughout my body from this blow.

I-330 quickly slipped down from his arms.

"Get away," she cried to R. "Don't you see, he's ... Get away, R, go!"

Baring his white, Negroid teeth, R spurted some word into my face, dived down, disappeared. And I lifted I-330 into my arms, pressed her firmly to myself, and carried her away.

My heart was throbbing—enormous—and with each heartbeat, a rush of such a riotous, hot wave of joy. And who cared if something somewhere had been smashed to bits—what did it matter! Only to carry her so, on and on ...

Evening. 22 O'clock.

It is with difficulty that I hold the pen in my hand: I am so exhausted after all the dizzying events of this morning. Is it possible that the sheltering, age-old walls of the One State have toppled? Is it possible that we are once again without house or roof, in the wild state of freedom, like our distant ancestors? Is there indeed no Benefactor? Against ... On Unanimity Day? I am ashamed, I am pained and frightened for them. But then, who

145

are "they"? And who am I? "They," "We"—do I know?

She sat on the sun-heated glass bench, on the topmost platform, where I had brought her. Her right shoulder and below—the beginning of the miraculous, incalculable curve—bare; the thinnest, serpentine, red trickle of blood. She did not seem to notice the blood, the bared breast . . . no, she saw it all—but this was precisely what she needed now, and if her unif were buttoned up, she would rip it open herself, she . . .

"And tomorrow . . ." she breathed greedily through gleaming, clenched, sharp teeth. "No one knows what tomorrow will be. Do you understand—I do not know, no one knows—tomorrow is the unknown! Do you understand that everything known is finished? Now all things will be new, unprecedented, inconceivable."

Below, the crowds were seething, rushing, screaming. But all that was far away, and growing farther, because she looked at me, she slowly drew me into herself through the narrow golden windows of her pupils. Long, silently. And for some reason I thought of how once, long ago, I had also stared through the Green Wall into someone's incomprehensible yellow eyes, and birds were circling over the Wall (or was this on some other occasion?).

"Listen: if nothing extraordinary happens tomorrow, I will take you there—do you understand?"

No, I did not understand. But I nodded silently. I was dissolved, I was infinitely small, I was a point. . . .

There is, after all, a logic of its own (today's logic) in this condition: a point contains more unknowns than anything else; it need but stir, move, and it may turn into thousands of curves, thousands of bodies.

I was afraid to stir: what would I turn into? And it seemed to me that everyone, like me, was terrified of the slightest movement.

At this moment, as I write this, everyone sits in his own glass cage, waiting for something. I do not hear the humming of the elevator usual at this hour, I hear no laughter, no steps. Now and then I see, in twos, glancing over their shoulders, people tiptoe down the corridor, whispering. . . .

What will happen tomorrow? What will I turn into tomorrow?

Twenty-sixth Entry

TOPICS: The World Exists
A Rash
41° Centigrade

Morning. Through the ceiling, the sky—firm, round, ruddy-cheeked as ever. I think I would be less astonished if I had seen above me some extraordinary square sun; people in varicolored garments of animal skins; stone, untransparent walls. Does it mean, then, that the world—our world—still exists? Or is this merely by inertia? The generator is already switched off, but the gears still clatter, turning—two revolutions, three, and on the fourth they'll stop. . . .

Are you familiar with this strange condition? You wake at night, open your eyes to blackness, and suddenly you feel you've lost your way—and quickly, quickly you grope around you, seeking something familiar, solid—a wall, a lamp, a chair. This was exactly how I groped around me, ran through the pages of the *One State Gazette*—quick, quick. And then:

Yesterday we celebrated Unanimity Day, which everyone has long awaited with impatience. For the forty-eighth time, the Benefactor, who has demonstrated his steadfast wisdom on so many past occasions, was elected by a unanimous vote. The celebration was marred by a slight disturbance, caused by the enemies of happiness. These enemies have, naturally, forfeited the right to serve as bricks in the foundation of the One State—a foundation renewed by yesterday's election. It is clear to everyone that taking account of their votes would be as absurd as considering the coughs of some sick persons in the audience as a part of a magnificent heroic symphony.

Oh, all-wise! Are we, after all, saved in spite of everything? Indeed, what objection can be raised to this most crystal clear of syllogisms?

And two lines further:

Today at twelve there will be a joint session of the Administrative Office, the Medical Office, and the Office of the Guardians. An important state action will take place within the next few days.

No, the walls are still intact. Here they are—I can feel them. And I no longer have that strange sensation that I am lost, that I am in some unknown place and do not know the way. And it's no longer surprising that I see the blue sky, the round sun. And everyone—as usual—is going to work.

I walked along the avenue with especially firm, ringing steps, and it seemed to me that everybody else walked with the same assurance. But when I turned at a crossing, I saw that everybody shied off sideways from the corner building, gave it a wide berth—as if a pipe had burst there and cold water were gushing out, making it impossible to use the sidewalk.

Another five, ten steps, and I was also showered with cold water, shaken, thrown off the sidewalk. ... At the height of some two meters a rectangular

149

sheet of paper was pasted on the wall, bearing an incomprehensible, venomously green inscription:

MEPHI

And beneath it, the S-shaped back, transparent wing-ears, quivering with anger, or excitement. His right hand raised, his left stretched helplessly back, like a hurt, broken wing, he was leaping up, trying to tear off the paper—and could not reach it, every time just short of touching it.

Each passerby was probably deterred by the same thought: If I come over, just I of all these others—won't he think I'm guilty of something and therefore trying ...

I confess to the same thought. But I recalled the many times when he was truly my Guardian Angel, the many times he saved me—and I boldly walked up to him, stretched my hand, and pulled off the sheet.

S turned, quickly bored his gimlets into me, to the very bottom, found something there. Then he raised his left eyebrow and winked with it at the wall where MEPHI had just hung. And flicked a corner of a smile at me, which seemed somehow astonishingly gay. But then, it was really nothing to wonder at. A physician will always prefer a rash and a forty-degree fever to the tormenting, slowly rising temperature of the incubation period: at least, the nature of the illness is clear. The MEPHI scattered on the walls today is the rash. I understood the smile.*

Steps down to the underground, and underfoot, on the immaculate glass of the stairs—again the

---

* I must confess that I discovered the true reason for this smile only after many days filled to the brim with the strangest and most unexpected events.

white sheet: MEPHI. And on the wall below, on a bench, on a mirror in the car (evidently pasted hurriedly, awry), everywhere the same white, frightening rash.

In the silence, the distinct hum of the wheels was like the noise of inflamed blood. Someone was touched on the shoulder; he started and dropped a roll of papers. And on my left, another—reading the same line in his newspaper over and over, the paper trembling faintly. I felt that everywhere—in the wheels, hands, newspapers, eyelashes—the pulse was beating faster and faster. And, perhaps, today, when I get there with I-330, the temperature will be thirty-nine, forty, forty-one degrees centigrade—marked on the thermometer by a black line. . . .

At the dock—the same silence, humming like a distant, invisible propeller. The machines stand glowering silently. And only the cranes are gliding, scarce audibly, as if on tiptoe, bending down, grasping in their claws the pale-blue blocks of frozen air and loading them into the tanks of the *Integral:* we are already preparing it for the test flight.

"Well, do you think we'll finish loading in a week?" I ask the Second Builder. His face is like fine china, embellished with sweet pale blue and delicately rosy flowers (eyes, lips) ; but today they are somehow faded, washed away. We calculate aloud, but I break off in the middle of a word and stand there, gaping: high under the cupola, on the blue block just lifted by the crane—a scarcely visible white square, a pasted sheet of paper. And all of me shakes—could it be with laughter? Yes, I hear myself laughing (do you know the feeling when you hear your own laughter?).

"No, listen. . . ." I say. "Imagine yourself in an ancient plane; the altimeter shows five thousand meters; the wing snaps, you plunge down like a tumbler pigeon, and on the way you calculate: 'Tomorrow, from twelve to two . . . from two to six . . . at six—dinner . . .' Isn't that absurd? But that's exactly what we are doing now!"

The little blue flowers stir, bulge. What if I were made of glass, and he could see that in some three or four hours . . .

Twenty-seventh Entry

TOPICS: None—Impossible

I am alone in endless corridors—the same ones, under the Ancient House. A mute, concrete sky. Water dripping somewhere on stone. Familiar, heavy, opaque door—and a muted hum behind it.

She said she would come out to me exactly at sixteen. But it is already five minutes past sixteen, ten, fifteen—no one.

For a second I am the old I, terrified that the door might open. Five more minutes, and if she does not come ...

Water dripping somewhere on stone. No one. With anguished joy I feel—I'm saved. I slowly walk back along the corridor. The quivering dotted line of bulbs on the ceiling grows dimmer and dimmer. ...

Suddenly, a door clicks hastily behind me, the quick patter of feet, softly rebounding from the walls, the ceiling—and there she is—light, airy, somewhat breathless with running, breathing through her mouth.

"I knew you would be here, you'd come! I knew—you, you ..."

The spears of her eyelashes spread open, they let me in—and ... How describe what it does to me—this ancient, absurd, miraculous ritual, when her lips touch mine? What formula can express the storm that sweeps everything out of my soul but her? Yes, yes, my soul—laugh if you will.

Slowly, with an effort, she raises her lids—and her words come slowly, with an effort. "No, enough ... later. Let us go now."

The door opens. Stairs—worn, old. And an intolerably motley noise, whistling, light ...

Nearly twenty-four hours have passed since then, and everything has settled down to some extent within me. And yet it is extremely difficult to describe what happened, even approximately. It is as if a bomb had been exploded in my head and open mouths, wings, shouts, leaves, words, rocks—piled, side by side, one after the other. ...

I remember my first thought was: Quick, rush back! It seemed clear to me: while I had waited in the corridor, they had managed somehow to blow up or destroy the Green Wall. And everything from out there had swept in and flooded our city, which had long ago been purged of the lower world.

I must have said something of the kind to I-330. She laughed. "Oh, no! We've simply come out beyond the Green Wall."

I opened wide my eyes: face to face with me, in wide-awake reality, was that which hitherto had not been seen by any living man except diminished a thousandfold, muted and dimmed by the thick, cloudy glass of the Wall.

The sun ... this was not our sun, evenly diffused over the mirror-smooth surface of our pavements.

154

These were living fragments, continually shifting spots, which dazed the eyes and made the head reel. And the trees, like candles—rising up into the sky itself; like spiders crouching on the earth with gnarled paws; like mute green fountains ... And everything was crawling, stirring, rustling. . . . Some shaggy little ball dashed out from underfoot. And I was frozen to the spot, I could not make a step, because under my feet was not a level surface—you understand—not a firm, level surface, but something revoltingly soft, yielding, springy, green, alive.

I was stunned by it all, I gasped, I gagged—perhaps this is the most accurate word. I stood, clutching at some swaying bough with both hands.

"It's nothing, it's nothing! It's only in the beginning, it will pass. Don't be afraid!"

Next to I-330, against the green, dizzyingly shifting latticework, somebody's finest profile, paper-thin. . . . No, not somebody's—I know him. I remember—it is the doctor. No, no, my mind is clear, I see everything. Now they are laughing; they have seized me by the arms and drag me forward. My feet get tangled, slip. Before us—moss, hillocks, screeching, cawing, twigs, tree trunks, wings, leaves, whistles. . . .

Then suddenly the trees spread out, run apart. A bright green clearing. In the clearing—people ... Or—I don't know what to call them—perhaps, more precisely, beings.

And here comes the most difficult part of all, because *this* transcended every limit of probability. And now it was clear to me why I-330 had always stubbornly refused to speak about it: I should not have believed her anyway—not even her. Perhaps, tomorrow I will not believe even myself—even these notes.

In the clearing, around a bare, skull-like rock,

there was a noisy crowd of three or four hundred
... people—I must say "people"—it is difficult to
call them anything else. Just as on the platforms in
our Plaza one sees at first only familiar faces, so
here I first saw only our gray-blue unifs. A second
more, and there, among the unifs, clearly and simply—black, red, golden, bay, roan, and white people—they must have been people. All were without
clothing and all were covered with short, glossy
fur, like the fur that can be seen by anyone on the
stuffed horse in the Prehistoric Museum. But the
females had faces exactly like those of our women:
delicately rosy and free of hair, as were also their
breasts—large, firm, of splendid geometric form.
The males had only parts of their faces hairless—
like our ancestors.

All this was so incredible, so unexpected, that I
stood calmly (yes, calmly!) and looked. It was the
same as with a scale: you overload one side, and
then, no matter how much more you add, the
arrow won't move.

Suddenly, I was alone. I-330 was no longer with
me—I didn't know where or how she had disappeared. Around me, only those beings, their furry
bodies glowing like satin in the sun. I seized someone's hot, firm, raven shoulder. "For the Benefactor's sake, tell me—where did she go? Why, just
now, just a moment ago ..."

Stern, shaggy eyebrows turned to me. "Sh-sh!
Quiet!" And he nodded shaggily toward the center
of the clearing, toward the yellow, skull-like stone.

There, above the heads, above everyone, I saw
her. The sun shone from behind her, directly into
my eyes, and all of her stood out sharp, coal-black
against the blue cloth of the sky—a charcoal silhou-
ette etched on blue. Just overhead, some clouds
floated by. And it seemed that not the clouds, but
the stone, and she herself, and with her the crowd

and the clearing were gliding as silently as a ship, and the earth itself, grown light, was floating underfoot. ...

"Brothers ..." She spoke. "Brothers! You all know: there, in the city behind the Wall, they are building the *Integral*. And you know: the day has come when we shall break down the Wall—all walls—to let the green wind blow free from end to end—across the earth. But the *Integral* is meant to take these walls up there, into the heights, to thousands of other earths, whose fires will rustle to you tonight through the black leaves. ..."

Waves, foam, wind against the stone: "Down with the *Integral*! Down!"

"No, brothers, not down. But the *Integral* must be ours. On the day when it first rises into the sky, we shall be in it. Because the Builder of the *Integral* is with us. He has come out from behind the Wall, he has come here with me, to be among you. Long live the Builder!"

A moment, and I was somewhere above. Beneath me—heads, heads, heads, wide-open shouting mouths, arms flashing up and falling. It was extraordinary, intoxicating: I felt myself above all others. I was I, a separate entity, a world. I had ceased to be a component, as I had been, and become a unit.

And now—with a dented, crumpled, happy body, as happy as after a love embrace—I am below, right near the stone. Sun, voices from above, I-330 smiling. A golden-haired, satiny-golden woman, spreading the fragrance of grass. In her hands, a cup, apparently of wood. She takes a sip from it with scarlet lips and hands it to me, and greedily, with closed eyes, to quench the fire, I drink the sweet, stinging, cold, fiery sparks.

And then—my blood and the whole world—a thousand times faster. The light earth flies like

157

down. And everything is light, and simple, and clear.

And now, I see the huge, familiar letters, MEPHI, on the stone, and for some reason this is right and necessary—it is the strong, simple thread that links everything together. I see a crude image—perhaps on the same stone: a winged youth with a transparent body and, where the heart should be, a dazzling, crimson-glowing coal. And again—I understand this coal. . . . Or no: I feel it—just as, without hearing, I feel every word (she is speaking from above, from the stone). And I feel that everybody breathes together—and everybody will fly together somewhere, like the birds over the Wall that day. . . .

From behind, from the densely breathing crowd of bodies—a loud voice: "But this is madness!"

And then it seems that I—yes, I believe it was I—jumped up on the stone. Sun, heads, a green serrated line against the blue, and I shout, "Yes, yes, madness! And everyone must lose his mind, everyone must! The sooner the better! It is essential—I know it."

Next to me, I-330. Her smile—two dark lines: from the ends of her lips—up, at an angle. And the coal is now within me, and all this is instant, easy, just a bit painful, beautiful. . . .

After that, only broken, separate fragments.

Slowly, just overhead—a bird. I see: it is alive, like me. Like a man it turns its head right, left, and black, round eyes drill into me. . . .

Another fragment: a back, with shiny fur the color of old ivory. A dark insect with tiny, transparent wings crawls along the back, and the back twitches to drive it off, then twitches again. . . .

Another fragment: the shadow of the leaves—interlaced, latticed. In the shadow people are lying and chewing something that resembles the legendary food of the ancients—a long yellow fruit and a piece of something dark. A woman thrusts it into my hand, and it is funny: I don't know whether I can eat it.

Again—a crowd, heads, feet, hands, mouths. Faces flash momentarily and disappear, burst like bubbles. And for a moment—or did it merely seem to me?—transparent, flying wing-ears.

With all my strength I press the hand of I-330. She glances back. "What is it?"

"He is here. . . . It seemed to me . . ."

"He? Who?"

"S . . . just a moment ago—in the crowd . . ."

The coal-black, thin eyebrows rise to the temples: sharp triangle, a smile. I do not understand why she is smiling; how can she smile?

"Don't you see—don't you see what it means if he or any of them is here?"

"Silly! Would it occur to anyone there, inside the Wall, that we are here? Try to remember—did you ever think that it was possible? They are hunting for us there—let them! You're dreaming."

She smiles lightly, gaily, and I smile. The earth—intoxicated, light, gay—floats. . . .

Twenty-eighth Entry

TOPICS: Two Women
Entropy and Energy
The Opaque Part of the Body

If your world is like the world of our distant forebears, imagine that you have stumbled upon a sixth, a seventh continent in the ocean—some Atlantis with fantastic labyrinth-cities, people soaring in the air without the aid of wings or aeros, rocks lifted by the power of a glance—in short, things that would never occur to you even if you suffer from dream-sickness. This is how I felt yesterday. Because, you understand—as I have told you before—not one of us has been beyond the Wall since the Two Hundred Years' War.

I know: it is my duty before you, my unknown friends, to tell in greater detail about the strange and unexpected world that revealed itself to me yesterday. But I am still unable to return to that. There is a constant flood of new and new events, and I cannot collect them all: I lift the edges of my unif, I hold out my palms, and yet whole pailfuls spill past, and only drops fall on these pages.

First I heard loud voices behind my door, and

recognized the voice of I-330, firm, metallic, and the other—almost inflexible, like a wooden ruler—the voice of U. Then the door flew open with a crash and catapulted both of them into my room. Yes, exactly—catapulted.

I-330 put her hand on the back of my chair and smiled at the other over her right shoulder, only with her teeth. I would not like to be faced with such a smile.

"Listen," I-330 said to me. "This woman, it appears, has set herself the task of protecting you from me, like a small child. Is that with your permission?"

And the other, her gills quivering, "Yes, he is a child. He is! That is the only reason he doesn't see that you're with him ... that it's only in order to ... that it is all a game. Yes. And it's my duty ..."

For a moment, in the mirror—the broken, jumping line of my eyebrows. I sprang up and, with difficulty restraining within me the other with the shaking hairy fists, with difficulty squeezing out each word through my teeth, I threw at her, straight at the gills, "Out! Th-this very moment! Get out!"

The gills swelled out, brick red, then drooped, turned gray. She opened her mouth to say something, then, saying nothing, snapped it shut and walked out.

I rushed to I-330. "I'll never—I'll never forgive myself! She dared—to you? But you don't think that I think, that ... that she ... It's all because she wants to register for me, and I ..."

"Fortunately, she won't have time to register. And I don't care if there are a thousand like her. I know you will believe me, not the thousand. Because, after what happened yesterday, I am open to you—all of me, to the very end, just as you wanted. I am in your hands, you can—at any moment ..."

"What do you mean—at any moment?" And immediately I understood. The blood rushed to my ears, my cheeks. I cried. "Don't, don't ever speak to me about it! You know that it was the other I, the old one, and now ..."

"Who can tell? A human being is like a novel: until the last page you don't know how it will end. Or it wouldn't be worth reading. ..."

She stroked my head. I could not see her face, but I could tell by her voice: she was looking far, far off, her eyes caught by a cloud, floating soundlessly, slowly, who knows where. . . .

Suddenly she thrust me away—firmly but tenderly. "Listen, I've come to tell you that these may be the last days we ... You know—the auditoriums have been canceled as of this evening."

"Canceled?"

"Yes. And as I walked past, I saw—they were preparing something in the auditoriums: tables, medics in white."

"But what can it mean?"

"I don't know. No one knows as yet. And that's the worst of it. But I feel—the current is switched on, the spark is running. If not today, then tomorrow. . . . But perhaps they won't have time enough."

I have long ceased to understand who "They" are, who are "We." I do not know what I want—whether I want them to have time enough, or not. One thing is clear to me: I-330 is now walking on the very edge—and any moment ...

"But this is madness," I say. "You—and the One State. It is like putting a hand over the muzzle of a gun and hoping to stop the bullet. It's utter madness!"

A smile. " 'Everyone must lose his mind—the
162

sooner the better.' Somebody said this yesterday. Do you remember? Out there . . ."

Yes, I have it written down. Hence, it really happened. Silently I stare into her face: the dark cross is especially distinct on it now.

"Darling, before it is too late . . . If you want, I will leave everything, I will forget it all—let's go together there, beyond the Wall, to those . . . whoever they are."

She shook her head. Through the dark windows of her eyes, deep within her, I saw a flaming oven, sparks, tongues of fire leaping up, a heaping pile of dry wood. And it was clear to me: it was too late, my words would no longer avail. . . .

She stood up. In a moment she would leave. These might be the last days—perhaps the last minutes. . . . I seized her hand.

"No! Just a little longer—oh, for the sake . . . for the sake . . ."

She slowly raised my hand, my hairy hand which I hated so much, toward the light. I wanted to pull it away, but she held it firmly.

"Your hand . . . You don't know—few know it—that there were women here, women of the city, who loved the others. You, too, must have some drops of sunny forest blood. Perhaps that's why I . . ."

A silence. And strangely—this silence, this emptiness made my heart race madly. And I cried, "Ah! You will not go! You will not go until you tell me about them, because you love . . . them, and I don't even know who they are, where they are from. Who are they? The half we have lost? H_2 and O? And in order to get H_2O—streams, oceans, waterfalls, waves, storms—the two halves must unite. . . ."

I clearly remember every movement she made. I remember how she picked up from the table my glass triangle, and while I spoke, she pressed its sharp edge to her cheek; there was a white line on the cheek, then it had filled with pink and vanished. And how strange that I cannot recall her words, especially at first—only fragmentary images, colors.

I know that in the beginning she spoke about the Two Hundred Years' War. I saw red on the green of grass, on dark clay, on blue snow—red, undrying pools. Then yellow, sun-parched grasses, naked, yellow, shaggy men and shaggy dogs—together, near swollen corpses, canine, or perhaps human. ... This, of course, outside the Wall. For the city had already conquered, the city had our present food, synthesized of petroleum.

And almost from the very sky, down to the ground—black, heavy, swaying curtains: slow columns of smoke, over woods, over villages. Stifled howling—black endless lines driven to the city—to be saved by force, to be taught happiness.

"You have almost known all this?"

"Yes, almost."

"But you did not know—few knew—that a small remnant still survived, remained there, outside the Wall. Naked, they withdrew into the woods. They learned how to live from trees, from animals and birds, from flowers and the sun. They have grown a coat of fur, but under the fur they have preserved their hot, red blood. With you it's worse: you're overgrown with figures; figures crawl all over you like lice. You should be stripped of everything and driven naked into the woods. To learn to tremble with fear, with joy, with wild rage, with cold, to pray to fire. And we, Mephi—we want ..."

"No, wait! 'Mephi'? What's 'Mephi'?"

"Mephi? It is an ancient name, it's he who ... Do you remember—out there, the image of the youth drawn on the stone? Or no, I'll try to say it in your language, it will be easier for you to understand. There are two forces in the world—entropy and energy. One leads to blissful quietude, to happy equilibrium; the other, to destruction of equilibrium, to tormentingly endless movement. Entropy was worshiped as God by our—or, rather, your—ancestors, the Christians. But we anti-Christians, we ..."

At this moment, there was a barely audible, a whispered knock at the door, and the man with the squashed face, with the forehead pushed low over his eyes, who had often brought me notes from I-330, burst into the room.

He rushed up to us, stopped, his breath hissing like an air pump, unable to say a word. He must have run at top speed.

"What is it! What happened?" She seized him by the hand.

"They're coming—here ..." he finally panted. "Guards ... and with them that—oh, what d'you call him ... like a hunchback ..."

"S?"

"Yes! They're right here, in the house. They'll be here in a moment. Quick, quick!"

"Nonsense! There's time. ..." She laughed, and in her eyes—sparks, gay tongues of flame.

It was either absurd, reckless courage—or something else, still unknown to me.

"For the Benefactor's sake! But you must realize—this is ..."

"For the Benefactor's sake?" A sharp triangle—a smile.

"Well, then ... for my sake ... I beg you."

"Ah, and I still had to talk to you about a certain matter. ... Oh, well, tomorrow ..."

She gaily (yes, gaily) nodded to me; the other, coming out for a fraction of a second from under his forehead, nodded too. And then I was alone.

Quick, to the table. I opened my notes, picked up a pen. They must find me at this work, for the benefit of the One State. And suddenly—every hair on my head came alive and separate, stirring: What if they take it and read at least one page—of these, the last ones?

I sat at the table, motionless—and saw the trembling of the walls, the trembling of the pen in my hands, the swaying, blurring of the letters. . . .

Hide it? But where? Everything is glass. Burn it? But they will see from the next rooms, from the hall. And then, I could not, I was no longer able to destroy this anguished—perhaps most precious—piece of myself.

From the distance, in the corridor, voices, steps. I only managed to snatch a handful of the sheets and thrust them under myself. And now I was riveted to the chair, which trembled with every atom. And the floor under my feet—a ship's deck. Up and down. . . .

Shrinking into a tiny lump, huddling under the shelter of my own brow, I saw stealthily, out of the corner of my eye, how they went from room to room, beginning at the right end of the hallway, and coming nearer, nearer. . . . Some sat benumbed, like me; others jumped up to meet them, throwing their doors wide open—lucky ones! If I could also . . .

"The Benefactor is the most perfect disinfection, essential to mankind, and therefore in the organism of the One State no peristalsis . . ." With a jumping pen I squeezed out this utter nonsense, bending ever lower over the table, while in my head there was a crazy hammering, and with my back I heard the door handle click. A gust of air. The chair under me danced. . . .

With an effort I tore myself away from the page and turned to my visitors. (How difficult it is to

play games. . . . Who spoke to me of games today?)
They were led by S. Glumly, silently, quickly his
eyes bored wells in me, in my chair, in the pages
quivering under my hand. Then, for a second—
familiar, everyday faces on the threshold, one sepa-
rating from among them—inflated, pink-brown
gills. . . .

I recalled everything that had taken place in this
room half an hour ago, and it was clear to me that
in a moment she . . . My whole being throbbed and
pulsed in that (fortunately, untransparent) part of
my body which covered the manuscript.

U approached S from behind, cautiously touched
his sleeve, and said in a low voice, "This is D-503,
the Builder of the *Integral*. You must have heard
of him. He is always working here, at his table. . . .
Doesn't spare himself at all!"

And I had . . . What an extraordinary, marvelous
woman.

S slid over to me, bent over my shoulder, over
the table. I tried to cover the writing with my
elbow, but he shouted sternly, "You will show me
what you have there, instantly!"

Flushed with shame, I held the paper out to
him. He read it, and I saw a smile slip out of his
eyes, flick down his face, and settle somewhere in
the right corner of his lips, with a faint quiver of
its tail. . . .

"Somewhat ambiguous. Nevertheless . . . Well,
continue: we shall not disturb you any more."

He plashed away, like paddles on water, toward
the door, and every step he made returned to me
gradually my feet, my hands, my fingers. My soul
again spread equally throughout my body. I was
able to breathe.

And the last thing: U lingered a moment in my
room, came over to me, bent to my ear, and in a
whisper, "It's your luck that I . . ."

What did she mean by that?

Later in the evening I learned that they had taken away three numbers. However, no one speaks aloud about this, or about anything that is happening these days (the educational influence of the Guardians invisibly present in our midst). Conversations deal chiefly with the rapid fall of the barometer and the change of weather.

TOPICS: Threads on the Face
Sprouts
Unnatural Compression

Strange: the barometer is falling, but there is still no wind. Quiet. Somewhere above, the storm that is still inaudible to us has started. Clouds are rushing madly. They are still few—separate jagged fragments. And it seems as if a city has already been overthrown up above, and pieces of walls and towers are tumbling down, growing before our eyes with terrifying speed—nearer and nearer; but they will still fly through blue infinity before they drop to the very bottom, where we are.

And here, below, there is silence. In the air—thin, incomprehensible, almost invisible threads. Every autumn they are carried here from outside, from beyond the Wall. Slowly, they float—and suddenly you feel something alien, invisible on your face; you want to brush it off, but no, you cannot; you cannot rid yourself of it.

There are especially many of these threads along the Green Wall, where I walked this morning. I-330 asked me to meet her in the Ancient House—in our old "apartment."

I was approaching the opaque mass of the Ancient House when I heard behind me someone's short, rapid steps and hurried breathing. I glanced back: O was trying to catch up with me.

All of her was firmly rounded in some special, somehow complete way. Her arms, the cups of her breasts, her entire body, so familiar to me, filled out, rounded, stretched her unif; in a moment, it seemed, they would break the thin cloth and burst into the sunlight. And I thought: Out there, in the green jungles, the sprouts push as stubbornly through the earth in spring—hurrying to send out branches, leaves, to bloom.

For several seconds she was silent, her blue eyes looking radiantly into my face.

"I saw you on Unanimity Day."

"I saw you too ..." And I remembered instantly how she had stood below, in the narrow passageway, pressing herself to the wall and shielding her stomach with her arms. Involuntarily, I glanced at it, round under the unif.

She evidently caught my glance. All of her turned roundly pink. A pink smile: "I am so happy, so happy ... I am full—you know, to the brim. I walk about and hear nothing around me, listening all the time within, inside me ..."

I was silent. There was something foreign on my face, disturbing, but I could not rid myself of it. Then suddenly, still glowing with blue radiance, she seized my hand—and I felt her lips on it. ... It was the first time in my life this happened to me. Some unknown, ancient caress—causing me such shame and pain that I (too roughly, perhaps) pulled away my hand.

"You've lost your mind! No, that isn't ... I mean, you ... Why such happiness? Have you forgotten what awaits you? If not now, in a month, in two months ..."

170

The light went out of her; all her roundness crumpled, shriveled at once. And in my heart—an unpleasant, a painful compression, connected with a sense of pity. (But the heart is nothing but an ideal pump; compression, shrinkage, the sucking in of fluid by a pump are technical absurdities. It is clear, then, how essentially preposterous, unnatural, and morbid are the "loves," "pities," and all the other nonsense that causes such compressions!)

Silence. On the left, the foggy green glass of the Wall. Ahead, the dark red massive house. And these two colors, adding up, produced within me what I thought a brilliant idea.

"Wait! I know how to save you. I'll free you of the need to die after seeing your child. You will be able to nurse it—you understand—you'll watch it grow in your arms, round out, fill up, and ripen like a fruit . . ."

She trembled violently and clutched at me.

"Do you remember that woman . . . that time, long ago, during our walk? Well, she is here now, in the Ancient House. Come with me to her; I promise, everything will be arranged at once."

I saw already in my mind's eye how, together with I-330, we led her through the corridors—I saw her there, among the flowers, grasses, leaves. . . . But she recoiled from me; the horns of her rosy crescent quivered and bent down.

"It's that one," she said.

"I mean . . ." I was embarrassed for some reason. "Well, yes, it is."

"And you want me to go to her—to ask her—to . . . Don't even dare to speak to me about it again!"

Stooping, she walked rapidly away. Then, as if suddenly remembering something, she turned and cried, "So I will die—I don't care! And it doesn't concern you—what does it matter to you?"

Silence. Pieces of blue walls and towers tumble from above, grow larger with terrifying speed, but they must still fly hours—perhaps days—through infinity. The invisible threads float slowly, settle on my face, and it's impossible to shake them off, to rid myself of them.

I slowly walk to the Ancient House. In my heart, an absurd, agonizing compression. ...

Thirtieth Entry

TOPICS : The Final Number
Galileo's Mistake
Would It Not Be Better?

Here is my conversation with I-330 yesterday, at the Ancient House, in the midst of motley, noisy colors—reds, greens, bronze-yellows, whites, oranges—stunning the mind, breaking up the logical flow of thought. . . . And all the time, under the frozen, marble smile of the pug-nosed ancient poet.

I reproduce this conversation to the letter—for it seems to me that it will be of vast, decisive importance to the destiny of the One State—nay, of the entire universe. Besides, perhaps, my unknown readers, you will find in it a certain vindication of me. . . .

I-330 flung everything at me immediately, without preliminaries. "I know: the *Integral* is to make its first, trial flight the day after tomorrow. On that day we shall seize it."

"What? The day after tomorrow?"

"Yes. Sit down, calm yourself. We cannot lose a minute. Among the hundreds rounded up at random by the Guardians last night there were twelve Mephi. If we delay a day or two, they'll perish."

I was silent.

"To observe the test, they have to send you electricians, mechanics, doctors, meteorologists. Exactly at twelve—remember this—when the lunch bell will ring and everyone will go to the dining room, we shall remain in the corridor, lock them in, and the *Integral* is ours.... Do you understand—it must be done, at any cost. The *Integral* in our hands will be the weapon that will help us finish everything quickly, painlessly, at once. Their aeros —ha! Insignificant gnats against a falcon. And then— if it becomes essential—we can simply direct the motor exhausts downward, and by their work alone ..."

I jumped up. "It's unthinkable! Absurd! Don't your realize that what you're planning is revolution?"

"Yes, revolution! Why is this absurd?"

"It is absurd because there can be no revolution. Because our—I am saying this, not you—our revolution was the final one. And there can be no others. Everyone knows this. ..."

The mocking, sharp triangle of eyebrows. "My dear—you are a mathematician. More—you are a philosopher, a mathematical philosopher. Well, then: name me the final number."

"What do you mean? I ... I don't understand: what final number?"

"Well, the final, the ultimate, the largest."

"But that's preposterous! If the number of numbers is infinite, how can there be a final number?"

"Then how can there be a final revolution? There is no final one; revolutions are infinite. The final one is for children: children are frightened by infinity, and it's important that children sleep peacefully at night ..."

"But what sense, what sense is there in all of

this—for the Benefactor's sake! What sense, if everybody is already happy?"

"Let us suppose ... Very well, suppose it's so. And what next?"

"Ridiculous! An utterly childish question. Tell children a story—to the very end, and they will still be sure to ask, 'And what next? And why?'"

"Children are the only bold philosophers. And bold philosophers are invariably children. Exactly, just like children, we must always ask, 'And what next?'"

"There's nothing next! Period. Throughout the universe—spread uniformly—everywhere. ..."

"Ah: uniformly, everywhere! That's exactly where it is—entropy, psychological entropy. Is it not clear to you, a mathematician, that only differences, differences in temperatures—thermal contrasts —make for life? And if everywhere, throughout the universe, there are equally warm, or equally cool bodies ... they must be brought into collision—to get fire, explosion, Gehenna. And we will bring them into collision."

"But I-330, you must understand—this was exactly what our forebears did during the Two Hundred Years' War. ..."

"Oh, and they were right—a thousand times right. But they made one mistake. They later came to believe that they had the final number—which does not, does not exist in nature. Their mistake was the mistake of Galileo: he was right that the earth revolves around the sun, but he did not know that the whole solar system also revolves— around some other center; he did not know that the real, not the relative, orbit of the earth is not some naïve circle ..."

"And you?"

"We? We know for the time being that there is no final number. We may forget it. No, we are
175

even sure to forget it when we get old—as everything inevitably gets old. And then we, too, shall drop—like leaves in autumn from the tree—like you, the day after tomorrow. ... No, no, my dear, not you. For you are with us, you are with us!"

Fiery, stormy, flashing—I have never yet seen her like that—she embraced me with all of herself. I disappeared. ...

At the last, looking firmly, steadily into my eyes, "Remember, then: at twelve."

And I said, "Yes, I remember."

She left. I was alone—among the riotous, many-voiced tumult of blue, red, green, bronze-yellow, orange colors. ...

Yes, at twelve ... And suddenly an absurd sensation of something alien settled on my face—impossible to brush off. Suddenly—yesterday morning, U—and what she had shouted into I-330's face. ... Why? What nonsense.

I hurried outside—and home, home. ...

Somewhere behind me I heard the piercing cries of birds over the Wall. And before me, in the setting sun—the spheres of cupolas, the huge, flaming cubes of houses, the spire of the Accumulator Tower like lightning frozen in the sky. And all this, all this perfect, geometric beauty will have to be ... by me, by my own hands ... Is there no way out, no other road?

Past one of the auditoriums (I forget the number). Inside it, benches piled up in a heap; in the middle, tables covered with sheets of pure white glass cloth; on the white, a stain of the sun's pink blood. And concealed in all of this—some unknown, and therefore frightening tomorrow. It is unnatural for a thinking, seeing being to live amidst irregulars, unknowns, X's ... As if you were blindfolded and forced to walk, feeling your way, stumbling, and knowing that somewhere—just nearby—is the edge; a single step, and all that will remain of you will be a flattened, mangled piece of flesh. Am I not like this now?

And what if—without waiting—I plunge myself, head down? Would it not be the only, the correct way—disentangling everything at once?

Thirty-first Entry

TOPICS: The Great Operation
I Have Forgiven Everything
A Train Collision

Saved! At the very last moment, when it seemed there was no longer anything to grasp at, when it seemed that everything was finished . . .

It is as though you have already ascended the stairs to the Benefactor's dread Machine, and the glass Bell has come down over you with a heavy clank, and for the last time in your life—quick, quick—you drink the blue sky with your eyes . . .

And suddenly—it was only a "dream." The sun is pink and gay, and the wall is there—what joy to stroke the cold wall with your hand; and the pillow—what an endless delight to watch and watch the hollow left by your head on the white pillow. . . .

This was approximately what I felt when I read the *One State Gazette* this morning. It had been a terrible dream, and now it was over. And I, faint-hearted nonbeliever, I had already thought of willful death. I am ashamed to read the last lines I had written yesterday. But it is all the same now:

let them stay as a reminder of the incredible thing that might have happened—and now will not happen ... no, it will not happen!

The front page of the *One State Gazette* glowed with a proclamation:

REJOICE!

For henceforth you shall be perfect! Until this day, your own creations—machines—were more perfect than you.

How?

Every spark of a dynamo is a spark of the purest reason; each movement of a piston is a flawless syllogism. But are you not possessors of the same unerring reason?

The philosophy of cranes, presses, and pumps, is as perfect and clear as a compass-drawn circle. Is your philosophy less compass-drawn?

The beauty of a mechanism is in its rhythm—as steady and precise as that of a pendulum. But you, nurtured from earliest infancy on the Taylor system—have you not become pendulum-precise?

Except for one thing:

Machines have no imagination.

Have you ever seen the face of a pump cylinder break into a distant, foolish, dreamy smile while it works? Have you ever heard of cranes restlessly turning from side to side and sighing at night, during the hours designated for rest?

No!

And you? Blush with shame! The Guardians have noticed more and more such smiles and sighs of late. And—hide your eyes—historians of the One State ask for retirement so that they need not record disgraceful events.

But this is not your fault—you are sick. The name of this sickness is

IMAGINATION.

It is a worm that gnaws out black lines on the forehead. It is a fever that drives you to escape ever farther, even if this "farther" begins where happiness ends. This is the last barricade on our way to happiness.

Rejoice, then: this barricade has already been blown up.

The road is open.

The latest discovery of State Science is the location of the center of imagination—a miserable little nodule in the brain in the area of the *pons Varolii*. Triple-X-ray cautery of this nodule—and you are cured of imagination—

FOREVER.

You are perfect. You are machinelike. The road to one hundred per cent happiness is free. Hurry, then, everyone—old and young—hurry to submit to the Great Operation. Hurry to the auditoriums, where the Great Operation is being performed. Long live the Great Operation! Long live the One State! Long live the Benefactor!

You ... If you were reading all this not in my notes, resembling some fanciful ancient novel, if this newspaper, still smelling of printers' ink, were trembling in your hands as it does in mine; if you knew, as I know, that this is the most actual reality, if not today's, then tomorrow's—would you not feel as I do? Wouldn't your head reel, as mine does? Wouldn't these eerie, sweet, icy needle pricks run down your back, your arms? Would it not seem to you that you're a giant, Atlas—and if you straighten up, you will inevitably strike the glass ceiling with your head?

I seized the telephone receiver. "I-330. ... Yes, yes, 330." And then I cried out breathlessly,

"You're home, yes? Have you read it? You're reading it? But this is, this is ... It's remarkable!"

"Yes. . . ." A long, dark silence. The receiver hummed faintly, pondered something. . . . "I must see you today. Yes, at my place, after sixteen. Without fail."

Dearest! Dear, such a dear! "Without fail ..." I felt myself smiling and could not stop. And now I would carry this smile along the street—high, like a light.

Outside, the wind swept at me. It whirled, howled, whipped, but I felt all the more exultant: whistle, scream—it doesn't matter now—you can no longer topple walls. And if cast-iron, flying clouds tumble overhead—let them tumble: they cannot blot out the sun. We have forever chained it to the zenith—we, Joshuas, sons of Nun.

At the corner a dense group of Joshuas stood with their foreheads glued to the glass wall. Inside, a man already lay stretched out on the dazzling white table. From under the white the bare soles of his feet formed a yellow angle; white doctors were bent over his head; a white hand stretched to another hand a hypodermic syringe filled with something.

"And you, why don't you go in?" I asked, addressing no one, or, rather, everyone.

"And what about you?" A spherical head turned to me.

"I will, later. I must first ..."

Somewhat embarrassed, I withdrew. I really had to see her, 330, first. But why "first"? This I could not answer.

The dock. Icy-blue, the *Integral* shimmered, sparkled. In the machine compartment the dynamo hummed gently, caressingly, repeating some word over and over again—and the word seemed familiar, one of my own. I bent over it and stroked the long, cold tube of the engine. Dear ... so dear. Tomorrow you will come alive; tomorrow, for the first time in your life, you will be shaken by the fiery, flaming sparks within your womb. ...

How would I be looking at this mighty glass monster if everything had remained as yesterday? If I knew that tomorrow at twelve I would betray it ... yes, betray. ...

Cautiously, someone touched my elbow from the back. I turned: the platelike flat face of the Second Builder.

"You know it already?" he said.

"What? The Operation? Yes? How strangely—everything, everything—at once ..."

"No, not that: the trial flight has been postponed to the day after tomorrow. All because of this Operation. ... And we were rushing, doing our best—and all for nothing. ..."

"All because of this Operation. ..." What a ridiculous, stupid man. Sees nothing beyond his flat face. If he only knew that, were it not for the Operation, he would be locked up in a glass box tomorrow at twelve, rushing about, trying to climb the walls ...

In my room, at half past fifteen. I entered and saw U. She sat at my table—bony, straight, rigid, her right cheek set firmly on her hand. She must have waited long, for, when she jumped up to meet me, five dents remained on her cheek from her fingers.

For a second I recalled that wretched morning, and herself there, raging by the table, next to I-330. ... But only for a second, and then the memory was washed away by today's sun. It was like entering the room on a bright day and absently turning the switch: the bulb lights up, but is invisible—pallid, absurd, unneeded. ...

Without a thought, I held my hand out to her, I

182

forgave her everything. She seized both of my hands and pressed them hard in her own bony ones. Her sagging cheeks quivering with excitement like some ancient ornaments, she said, "I have been waiting . . . Only for a moment. . . . I only wanted to say how happy I am, how glad for you! You understand—tomorrow, or the day after, you will be well—completely well, newly born. . . .

I saw some sheets of paper on the table—the last pages of my notes. They lay there as I left them in the evening. If she had seen what I had written there . . . However, it no longer mattered; now it was merely history, ridiculously distant, like something seen through the wrong end of binoculars. . . .

"Yes," I said. "And you know—just now I was walking down the street, and there was a man before me, and his shadow on the pavement. And imagine, the shadow glowed. And it seems to me—I am certain—that tomorrow there will be no shadows. No man, no object will cast a shadow. . . . The sun will shine through everything . . ."

She spoke gently and sternly. "You are a dreamer! I would not permit the children at school to speak like that. . . ."

And she went on about the children—how she had taken them all to the Operation, and how they had had to be tied up there . . . and that "love must be ruthless, yes, ruthless," and that she thought she would at last decide . . .

She smoothed the gray blue cloth over her knees, quickly and silently plastered me over with her smile, and left.

Fortunately, the sun had not yet stopped today; it was still running, and now it was sixteen. I knocked at the door, my heart beating. . . .

"Come in!"

And I was down on the floor near her chair,

183

embracing her legs, head thrown back and looking into her eyes—one, then the other—and in each one seeing myself, in marvelous captivity. . . .

And then, outside the wall, a storm. Clouds darkening—more and more like cast iron. Let them! My head could not contain the flow of riotous, wild words—spilling over the rim. I spoke aloud, and, together with the sun, we were flying somewhere . . . But now we knew where—and behind us, planets—planets spraying flame, inhabited by fiery, singing flowers—and mute, blue planets, where sentient, rational stones were organized into societies—planets which, like our earth, had reached the summit of absolute, and hundred per cent happiness. . . . .

Suddenly, from above, "But don't you think that the society at the summit is precisely a society organized of stones?" The triangle of her eyebrows grew sharper, darker. "And happiness ... Well, after all, desires torment us, don't they? And, clearly, happiness is when there are no more desires, not one . . . What a mistake, what ridiculous prejudice it's been to have marked happiness always with a plus sign. Absolute happiness should, of course, carry a minus sign—the divine minus."

I remember I muttered in confusion, "Absolute minus? Minus 273° . . ."

"Precisely—minus 273°. Somewhat chilly, but wouldn't that in itself prove that we're at the summit?"

As once, a long time ago, she somehow spoke for me, through me, unfolding my ideas to the very end. But there was something sharply frightening in it—I could not bear it, and with an effort I forced a "no" out of myself.

"No," I said. "You ... you are mocking me. . . ."

She laughed, loudly—too loudly. Quickly, in a

second, she laughed herself to some unseen edge, stumbled, fell. ... A silence.

She rose and placed her hands upon my shoulders, and looked at me slowly and long. Then pulled me to herself—and there was nothing, only her hot, sharp lips.

"Farewell!"

It came from far, from above, and took a long time to reach me—a minute, perhaps, or two.

"What do you mean, 'Farewell'?"

"Well, you are sick, you have committed crimes because of me—has it not been a torment to you? And now, the Operation—and you will cure yourself of me. And that means—farewell."

"No," I cried out.

A pitilessly sharp, dark triangle on white: "What? You don't want happiness?"

My head was splitting; two logical trains collided, climbing upon each other, crashing, splintering. ...

"Well, I am waiting. Make your choice: the Operation and one hundred per cent happiness— or ..."

"I cannot ... without you. I want nothing without you," I said, or merely thought—I am not sure—but she heard.

"Yes, I know," she answered. And, her hands still on my shoulders, her eyes still holding mine, "Until tomorrow, then. Tomorrow, at twelve. You remember?"

"No, it's been postponed for a day. ... The day after tomorrow. ..."

"All the better for us. At twelve, the day after tomorrow. ..."

I walked alone through the twilit street. The wind was whirling, driving, carrying me like a slip of paper. Fragments of cast-iron sky flew and flew—

they had another day, two days to hurtle through infinity. ... The unifs of passersby brushed against me, but I walked alone. I saw it clearly: everyone was saved, but there was no salvation for me. *I did not want salvation. ...*

Thirty-second Entry

TOPICS: I Do Not Believe
Tractors
A Human Splinter

Do you believe that *you will die?* Yes, man is mortal, I am a man: hence ... No, this is not what I mean. I know you know this. I am asking: have you ever really believed it; believed it totally, not with your mind, but with your *body;* have you ever felt that one day the fingers holding this very page will be icy, yellow. ...

No, of course you don't believe it—and this is why you have not jumped from the tenth floor down to the pavement; this is why you are still eating, turning the page, shaving, smiling, writing. ...

The same—yes, exactly the same—is true of me today. I know that this little black arrow on the clock will crawl down here, below, to midnight, will slowly rise again, will step across some final line—and the incredible tomorrow will be here. I know this, but somehow I also *don't believe it*. Or, perhaps, it seems to me that twenty-four hours are twenty-four years. And this is why I can still do something, hurry somewhere, answer questions, climb the ladder to the *Integral*. I still feel it rocking on the water; I know I must grasp the handrail and feel the cold glass under my hand. I see the transparent, living cranes bend their long, birdlike necks, stretch their beaks, and tenderly, solicitously feed the *Integral* with the terrible explosive food for its motors. And below, on the river, I clearly see the blue, watery veins and nodes, swollen with the wind. But all of this is quite apart from me, extraneous, flat—like a scheme on a sheet of paper. And it is strange that the flat, paper face of the Second Builder is suddenly speaking.

"Well, then? How much fuel shall we take for the motors? If we think of three ... or three and a half hours ..."

Before me—projected on the blueprint—my hand with the calculator, the logarithmic dial at fifteen.

"Fifteen tons. No, better load ... yes—load a hundred ..."

Because, after all, I do know that tomorrow ...

And I see, from somewhere at the side: my hand with the dial starts to tremble faintly.

"A hundred? Why so much? That would be for a week. A week? Much longer!"

"Anything might happen. ... Who knows ..." I know ...

The wind howls; the air is tightly filled with something invisible, to the very top. I find it hard to breathe, hard to walk. And slowly, with an effort, without stopping for a second, the arrow crawls upon the face of the clock on the Accumulator Tower at the end of the avenue. The spire is in the clouds—dim, blue, howling in muted tones, sucking electricity. The trumpets of the Music Plant howl.

As ever, in rows, four abreast. But the rows are somehow unsolid; perhaps it is the wind that makes them waver, bend—more and more. Now

188

they have collided with something on the corner, they flow back, and there is a dense, congealed, immobile cluster, breathing rapidly. Suddenly everyone is craning his neck.

"Look! No, look—that way, quick!"

"It's they! It's they!"

"... I'll never ... Better put my head straight into the Machine. ..."

"Sh-sh! You're mad. ..."

In the auditorium at the corner the door is gaping wide, and a slow, heavy column of some fifty people emerges. "People?" No, that does not describe them. These are not feet—they are stiff, heavy wheels, moved by some invisible transmission belt. These are not people—they are humanoid tractors. Over their heads a white banner is flapping in the wind, a golden sun embroidered on it; between the sun's rays, the words: "We are the first! We have already undergone the Operation! Everybody, follow us!"

Slowly, irresistibly, they plow through the crowd. And it is clear that, if there were a wall, a tree, a house in their way, they would without halting plow through the wall, the tree, the house. Now they are in the middle of the avenue. Hands locked, they spread out into a chain, facing us. And we—a tense knot, necks stretched, heads bristling forward—wait. Clouds. Whistling wind.

Suddenly the flanks of the chain, on the right and the left, bend quickly and rush upon us, faster, faster, like a heavy machine speeding downhill. They lock us in the ring—and toward the gaping doors, into the doors, inside ..

Someone's piercing scream: "They're driving us in! Run!"

And everybody rushes. Just near the wall there is still a narrow living gateway, and everyone streams there, head forward—heads instantly sharp as

189

wedges, sharp elbows, shoulders, sides. Like a jet of water, compressed inside a fire hose, they spread fanlike, and all around—stamping feet, swinging arms, unifs. From somewhere for an instant—a glimpse of a double curved, S-like body, translucent wing-ears—and he is gone, as though swallowed by the earth, and I am alone, in the midst of flashing arms and feet—I run. . . .

I dive into a doorway for a moment's breath, my back pressed to the door—and instantly, a tiny human splinter—as if driven to me by the wind.

"I was . . . following you . . . all the time . . . I do not want to—you understand—I do not want to. I agree. . . ."

Round, tiny hands upon my sleeve, round blue eyes: it is O. She seems to slide down along the wall and slump onto the ground. Shrunk into a little ball below, on the cold stair, and I bend over her, stroking her head, her face—my hands are wet. As though I were very big, and she—altogether tiny—a tiny part of my own self. This is very different from the feeling for I-330. It seems to me that something like it may have existed among the ancients toward their private children.

Below, through the hands covering the face, just audibly: "Every night I . . . I cannot . . . if they cure me . . . Every night—alone, in darkness—I think about him: what he will be like, how I will . . . There will be nothing for me to live by—you understand? And you must, you must . . ."

A preposterous feeling, but I know: yes, I must. Preposterous, because this duty of mine is yet another crime. Preposterous, because white cannot at the same time be black, duty and crime cannot coincide. Or is there no black or white in life, and the color depends only on the initial logical premise? And if the premise was that I unlawfully gave her a child . . .

190

"Very well—but don't, don't . . ." I say. "You understand, I must take you to I-330—as I offered that time—so that she . . ."

"Yes." Quietly, without taking her hands from her face.

I helped her to get up. And silently, each with our own thoughts—who knows, perhaps about the same thing—along the darkening street, among mute, leaden houses, through the taut, swishing branches of wind . . .

At a certain transparent, tense point, I heard through the whistling of the wind familiar, slapping steps. At the corner, I glanced back, and in the midst of the rushing, upside-down clouds reflected in the dim glass of the pavement I saw S. Immediately, my hands were not my own, swinging out of time, and I was telling O loudly that tomorrow—yes, tomorrow—the *Integral* would go up for the first time, and it would be something utterly unprecedented, uncanny, miraculous.

O gave me an astonished, round, blue stare, looked at my loudly, senselessly swinging arms. But I did not let her say a word—I shouted on and on. And there, within me, separately—heard only by myself—the feverish, humming, hammering thought, No, I must not . . . I must somehow . . . I must not lead him to I-330 . . .

Instead of turning left, I turned right. The bridge offered its obedient, slavishly bent back to the three of us—to me, O, and to S—behind us. The brightly lit buildings on the other side scattered lights into the water, the lights broke into thousands of feverishly leaping sparks, sprayed with frenzied white foam. The wind hummed like a thick bass string stretched somewhere low overhead. And through the bass, behind us all the time . . .

The house where I live. At the door O stopped, began to say something. "No! You promised . . ."

I did not let her finish. Hurriedly I pushed her into the entrance, and we were in the lobby, inside. Over the control desk, the familiar, excitedly quivering, sagging cheeks. A dense cluster of numbers in heated argument; heads looking over the banister from the second floor; people running singly down the stairs. But I would see about that later, later . . . Now I quickly drew O into the opposite corner, sat down, back against the wall (behind the wall I saw, gliding back and forth, a dark, large-headed shadow), and took out a note pad.

O slowly sagged into her chair—as though her body were melting, evaporating under her unif, and there were only an empty unif and empty eyes that sucked you into their blue emptiness.

Wearily, "Why did you bring me here? You lied to me!"

"No . . . Be quiet! Look that way—you see, behind the wall?"

"Yes, A shadow."

"He follows me all the time . . . I cannot. You understand—I must not. I'll write two words—you'll take the note and go alone. I know he will remain here."

The body stirred again under the unif, the belly rounded out a little; on the cheeks—a faint, rosy dawn.

I slipped the note into her cold fingers, firmly pressed her hand, dipped my eyes for the last time into her blue eyes.

"Good-by! Perhaps, some day we shall . . ."

She took away her hand. Stooping, she walked off slowly. . . . Two steps, and quickly she turned—and was again next to me. Her lips moved. With her eyes, her lips, all of herself—a single word, saying a single word to me—and what an unbearable smile, what pain. . . .

And then, a bent tiny human splinter in the doorway, a tiny shadow behind the wall—without looking back, quickly, ever more quickly . . .

I went over to U's desk. Excitedly, indignantly inflating her gills, she said to me, "You understand—they all seem to have lost their heads! He insists that he has seen some human creature near the Ancient House—naked and all covered with fur . . ."

From the dense cluster of heads, a voice: "Yes! I'll say it again—I saw it, yes."

"Well, what do you think of that? The man's delirious!"

And this "delirious" of hers was so sure, so unbending that I asked myself: Perhaps all of it, all that's been happening to me and around me lately is really nothing but delirium?

But then I glanced at my hairy hands, and I remembered: "There must be a drop of forest blood in you . . . Perhaps that's why I . . ."

No—fortunately, it is not delirium. No—unfortunately, it is not delirium.

The day has come.

Quick, the newspaper. Perhaps it . . . I read it with my eyes (precisely—my eyes are now like a pen, a calculator, which you hold in your hands and feel—it is apart from you, an instrument).

In bold type, across the front page:

> The enemies of happiness are not sleeping. Hold on to your happiness with both hands! Tomorrow all work will halt—all numbers shall report for the Operation. Those who fail to do so will be subject to the Benefactor's Machine.

Tomorrow! Can there be—will there be a tomorrow?

By daily habit, I stretch my hand (an instrument) to the bookshelf to add today's *Gazette* to the others, in the binding stamped with the gold design. And on the way: What for? What does it matter? I shall never return to this room.

The newspaper drops to the floor. And I stand up and look around the room, the whole room; I hastily take with me, gather up into an invisible valise, all that I'm sorry to leave behind. The table. The books. The chair. I-330 sat in it that day, and I—below, on the floor . . . The bed . . .

Then, for a minute or two—absurdly waiting for some miracle. Perhaps the telephone will ring, perhaps she'll say that . . .

No. There is no miracle.

I am leaving—into the unknown. These are my last lines. Good-by, beloved readers, with whom I've lived through so many pages, to whom, having contracted the soul sickness, I have exposed all of myself, to the last crushed little screw, the last broken spring . . .

I am leaving.

Thirty-fourth Entry

TOPICS: The Excused Ones
Sunny Night
Radio Valkyrie

Oh, if I had really smashed myself and all the others to smithereens, if I had really found myself with her somewhere behind the Wall, among beasts baring their yellow fangs, if I had never returned here! It would have been a thousand, a million times easier. But now—what? To go and strangle that ... But how would that help?

No, no, no! Take yourself in hand, D-503. Set yourself upon some firm logical axis—if only for a short time, bear down on the lever with all your strength, and, like an ancient slave, turn the millstones of syllogisms—until you write down, think over everything that happened. ...

When I boarded the *Integral*, everybody was already there, each at his post; all the cells in the gigantic glass beehive were full. Through the glass decks—tiny human ants below, near the telegraphs, dynamos, transformers, altimeters, valves, indicators, engines, pumps, tubes. In the lounge—a group of unknown men over schemes and instruments, probably assigned there by the Scientific Bureau.

196

And with them, the Second Builder with two of his assistants.

All three with their heads drawn, turtlelike, into their shoulders, their faces—gray, autumnal, joyless.

"Well?" I asked.

"Oh ... A bit nervous ..." one of them said with a gray, lusterless smile. "Who knows where we may have to land? And generally, it's uncertain ..."

It was unbearable to look at them—at those whom I would in an hour, with my own hands, eject from the comfortable figures of the Table of Hours, tearing them away from the maternal breast of the One State. They reminded me of the tragic figures of the "Three Excused Ones," whose story is known to every schoolboy. It is a story of how three numbers were, by way of an experiment, excused from work for a month: do what you like, go where you wish.* The wretches loitered near their usual places of work, peering inside with hungry eyes; they stood in the street hour after hour, repeating the motions which had already become necessary to their organisms at the given times of day: they sawed and planed the air, swung invisible hammers, struck invisible blocks. And, finally, on the tenth day, unable to endure it any longer, they linked hands, walked into the water, and to the sounds of the March, went deeper and deeper, until the water put an end to their misery. . . .

I repeat: it was painful for me to look at them; I hurried to leave them.

"I will check the machine compartment," I said, "and then—we're off."

They asked me questions: what voltage was to

---

* This happened long ago, in the third century after the introduction of the Table.

be used for the starting blast, how much water ballast for the stern tank. There was a phonograph inside me: it answered all questions promptly and precisely, while I continued inwardly without interruption with my own thoughts.

Suddenly, in a narrow passageway, something reached me, within—and from that moment it all began.

In the narrow passageway gray unifs, gray faces flickered past me, and, for a second, one face: hair low on the forehead, deep-set eyes—that same man. I understood: they were here, and there was no escape from all this anywhere, and only minutes remained—a few dozen minutes. . . . The tiniest molecular shivers ran through my body (they did not stop to the very end)—as though a huge motor had been set up within me, and the structure of my body was too slight for it, and so the walls, the partitions, the cables, the beams, the lights—everything trembled. . . .

I did not know yet whether she was there. But there was no more time now—I was called upstairs, to the command cabin: it was time to go. . . . Where?

Gray, lusterless faces. Tense blue veins below, in the water. Heavy, cast-iron layers of sky. And how hard to lift my cast-iron hand, to pick up the receiver of the command telephone.

"Up—45 degrees!"

A dull blast—a jolt—a frenzied white-green mountain of water aft—the deck slipping away from underfoot—soft, rubbery—and everything below, all of life, forever . . . For a second we were falling deeper and deeper into some funnel, and everything contracted: the icy-blue relief map of the city, the round bubbles of its cupolas, the solitary leaden finger of the Accumulator Tower. Then a momentary cottonwool curtain of clouds—

we plunged through it—sun and blue sky. Seconds, minutes, miles—the blue was rapidly congealing, filling up with darkness, and stars emerged like drops of silvery, cold sweat. . . .

And now—the uncanny, intolerably bright, black, starry, sunny night. It was like suddenly becoming deaf: you still see the roaring trumpets, but you only see them: the trumpets are mute, all is silence. The sun was mute.

All this was natural, it was to be expected. We had left the earth's atmosphere. But everything had happened so quickly, had taken everyone so unawares, that everyone around was cowed, silenced. And to me—to me it all seemed easier somehow under this mute, fantastic sun: as though, crumpling up for the last time, I had already crossed the inescapable threshold—and my body was somewhere there, below, while I sped through a new world where everything must be so unfamiliar, so upside down. . . .

"Hold the course!" I shouted into the receiver. Or, perhaps, it was not I, but the phonograph in me—and with a mechanical, hinged hand I thrust the command phone into the hands of the Second Builder. And I, shaken from head to foot by the finest molecular trembling, which I alone could feel, ran downstairs, to look for . . .

The door to the lounge—the one that in an hour would heavily click shut. . . . By the door, someone I did not know—short, with a face like hundreds, thousands of others, a face that would be lost in a crowd. And only his hands were unusual—extraordinarily long, down to his knees, as though taken in a hurry, by mistake, from another human set.

A long arm stretched out, barred the way. "Where to?"

Clearly, he did not know that I knew everything.

Very well: perhaps this was as it should be. And looking down on him, deliberately curt, I said, "I am the Builder of the *Integral*. I supervise the tests. Understand?"

The arm was gone.

The lounge. Over the instruments and maps—gray, bristly heads, and yellow heads, bald, ripe. Quickly, I swept them with a glance, and back, along the corridor, down the hatch, to the engine room. Heat and din of pipes red-hot from the explosions, cranks gleaming in a desperate, drunken dance, the incessant, faintly visible quiver of arrows on the dials. . . .

And finally, at the tachometer—he, with the low forehead bent over a notebook. . . .

"Listen . . ." The din made it necessary to shout into his ear. "Is she here? Where is she?"

In the shadow under the forehead, a smile. "She? There, in the radio-telephone room. . . ."

I rushed in. There were three of them, all in winged receiving helmets. She seemed a head taller than ever, winged, gleaming, flying—like the ancient Valkyries. And the huge blue sparks above, over the radio antenna, seemed to come from her, and the faint, lightning smell of ozone, also from her.

"Someone . . . no—you . . ." I said to her breathlessly (from running). "I must transmit a message down, to the earth, to the dock. . . . Come, I'll dictate it. . . ."

Next to the apparatus room there was a tiny boxlike cabin. Side by side, at the table. I found her hand, pressed it hard. "Well? What next?"

"I don't know. Do you realize how wonderful it is to fly, not knowing where—to fly—no matter where . . . And soon it will be twelve—and who knows what's to come? And night. . . . Where shall we be at night, you and I? Perhaps on grass, on dry leaves . . ."

She emanates blue sparks and smells of lightning, and my trembling grows more violent.

"Write down," I say loudly, still out of breath (with running). "Time, eleven-thirty. Velocity: sixty-eight hundred . . ."

She, from under the winged helmet, without taking her eyes from the paper, quietly: "She came to me last night with your note. . . . I know—I know everything, don't speak. But the child is yours? And I sent her there—she is already safe, beyond the Wall. She'll live. . . ."

Back in the commander's cabin. Again—the night, delirious, with a black starry sky and dazzling sun; the clock hand on the wall—limping slowly, from minute to minute; and everything as in a fog, shaken with the finest, scarcely perceptible (perceptible to me alone) trembling.

For some reason, it seemed to me: It would be better if all that was about to follow took place not here, but lower, nearer to the earth.

"Halt engines!" I cried into the receiver.

Still moving by inertia, but slower, slower. Now the *Integral* caught at some hair-thin second, hung for a moment motionless; then the hair broke, and the *Integral* plunged like a stone—down, faster, faster. And so, in silence, for minutes, dozens of minutes, I heard my own pulse. The clock hand before my eyes crawled nearer and nearer to twelve. And it was clear to me: I was the stone; I-330 was the earth, and I—a stone, thrown by someone's hand. And the stone was irresistibly compelled to fall, to crash against the earth, to smash itself to bits. . . . And what if . . . Below, the hard blue smoke of clouds was already visible. . . . What if . . .

But the phonograph inside me picked up the

receiver with hingelike precision, gave the command: "Low speed." The stone no longer fell. And now only the four lower auxiliaries—two fore, two aft—puffed wearily, merely to neutralize the *Integral*'s weight, and the *Integral* stopped in mid-air with a slight quiver, firmly anchored, about a kilometer from the earth.

Everyone rushed out on deck (it's almost twelve—time for the lunch bell) and, bending over the glass railing, hurriedly gulped the unknown world below, beyond the Wall. Amber, green, blue: the autumn woods, meadows, a lake. At the edge of a tiny blue saucer, some yellow, bonelike ruins, a threatening, yellow, dry finger—probably the spire of an ancient church, miraculously preserved.

"Look, look! There, to the right!"

There—in a green wilderness—a rapid spot flew like a brown shadow. I had binoculars in my hand; mechanically I brought them to my eyes: chest-deep in the grass, with sweeping tails, a herd of brown horses galloped, and on their backs, those beings—bay, white, raven black. . . .

Behind me: "And I tell you—I saw a face."

"Go on! Tell it to someone else!"

"Here, here are the binoculars. . . ."

But they were gone now. And endless green wilderness . . .

And in the wilderness—filling all of it, and all of me, and everyone—the piercing quaver of a bell: lunchtime, in another minute, at twelve.

The world—scattered in momentary, unconnected fragments. On the steps, somebody's clanking golden badge—and I don't care: it crunched under my heel. A voice: "And I say, there was a face!" A dark rectangle: the open door of the lounge. Clenched, white, sharply smiling teeth. . . .

And at the moment when the clock began to strike, with agonizing slowness, without breathing from one stroke to the next, and the front ranks had already begun to move—the rectangle of the door was suddenly crossed over by two familiar, unnaturally long arms:

"Stop!"

Fingers dug into my palm—I-330, next to me.

"Who is he? Do you know him?"

"Isn't he ... Isn't he one of ..."

He stood on someone's shoulders. Over a hundred faces—his face, like hundreds, thousands of others, yet unique.

"In the name of the Guardians ... Those to whom I speak, they hear me, each of them hears me. I say to you—we know. We do not know your numbers as yet, but we know everything. The *Integral* shall not be yours! The test flight will be completed; and you—you will not dare to make a move now—you will do it, with your own hands. And afterward ... But I have finished. ..."

Silence. The glass squares underfoot are soft as cotton; my feet are soft as cotton. She is beside me—utterly white smile, frenzied blue sparks. Through her teeth, into my ear, "Ah, so you did it? You 'fulfilled your duty'? Oh, well ..."

Her hand broke from my hand, the Valkyrie's wrathful, winged helmet was now somewhere far ahead. Alone, silent, frozen, I walked like all the others into the lounge. ...

But no, it wasn't I—not I! I spoke of it to no one, no one except those white, mute pages ... Within me—inaudibly, desperately, loudly—I cried this to her. She sat across the table, opposite me, and she did not once allow her eyes to touch me. Next to her, someone's ripe-yellow bald head.

I heard (it was I-330 speaking), " 'Nobility?' No, my dearest Professor, even a simple philological analysis of the word will show that it is nothing but a relic of ancient feudal forms. And we ..."

I felt myself go pale—and now everyone would see it . . . But the phonograph within me performed the fifty prescribed masticating movements for every bite, I locked myself within me as in an ancient, untransparent house—I piled rocks before my door, I pulled down the shades . . .

Later—the commander's receiver in my hands; and flight, in icy, final anguish—through clouds—into the icy, starry-sunny night. Minutes, hours. And evidently all this time, at feverish speed, the logical motor, unheard even by me, continued to work within me. For suddenly, at a certain point of blue space, I saw: my writing table, and over it U's gill-like cheeks, and the forgotten pages of my notes. And it was clear to me: no one but she—everything was clear. . . .

Ah, if I could only . . . I must, I must get to the radio room . . . The winged helmets, the smell of blue lightning . . . I remember—I was speaking to her loudly. And I remember—looking through me as though I were of glass—from far away, "I am busy. I am receiving messages from below. Dictate to her. . . ."

In the tiny cabin, after a moment's thought, I dictated firmly, "Time—fourteen-forty. Down! Stop engines. The end of everything."

The command cabin. The *Integral*'s mechanical heart has been stopped, we are dropping, and my heart cannot keep up; it falls behind, it rises higher and higher into my throat. Clouds—then a distant green spot—ever greener, clearer—rushing madly at us—now—the end . . .

The white-porcelain twisted face of the Second Builder. It must be he who pushed me with all his strength. My head struck something, and falling, darkening, I heard as through a fog, "Aft engines—full speed!"

A sharp leap upward . . . I remember nothing else.

Thirty-fifth Entry

TOPICS: In a Hoop
A Carrot
A Murder

I did not sleep all night. All night—a single thought ...

Since yesterday, my head is tightly bandaged. But no: it's not a bandage—it is a hoop; a merciless tight hoop of glass steel riveted to my head, and I am caught within this single, locked circle: I must kill U. Kill her, and then go to the other and say, "Now you believe?" The most disgusting thing of all is that killing is somehow messy, primitive. Crushing her skull with something—it gives me a strange sensation of something sickeningly sweet in the mouth, and I cannot swallow my saliva, I keep spitting it out into my handkerchief, and my mouth is dry.

In my closet there was a heavy piston rod which had snapped in the casting (I had to examine the structure of the breach under the microscope). I rolled up my notes into a tube (let her read all of me—to the last letter), slipped the rod into the tube, and went downstairs. The staircase was interminable, the stairs disgustingly slippery, liquid; I wiped my lips with my handkerchief all the time. . . .

Below. My heart thumped. I stopped, pulled out the rod, and walked to the control table. . . .

U was not there: an empty, icy board. I remembered—all work was stopped today; everyone was to report for the Operation. Of course, there was no reason for her to be here—no one to register.

In the street. Wind. A sky of flying cast-iron slabs. And—as at a certain moment yesterday—the world was split into sharp, separate, independent fragments, and each, as it hailed down, halted for a second, hung before me in the air—and vanished without a trace.

It was as though the precise, black letters on this page were suddenly to slide off, scatter in terror—here, there—and not a single word, nothing but a senseless jumble: fright-skip-jump. . . . The crowd in the street was also like that—scattered, not in rows—moving forward, back, aslant, across.

And now no one. And for an instant, rushing headlong, everything stood still. There, on the second floor, in a glass cage suspended in the air, a man and a woman—kissing as they stood, her whole body brokenly bent backward. This— forever, for the last time. . . .

At some corner, a stirring, spiky bush of heads. Over the heads—separately, in the air—a banner, words: "Down with the machines! Down with the Operation!" And apart (from me) —I, with a fleeting thought: Is everybody filled with pain that can be torn from within only together with his heart? Must everybody do something, before . . . And for a second there was nothing in the world except my brutish hand with its heavy, cast iron roll. . . .

A small boy—all of him thrust forward, a shadow under his lower lip. The lower lip is turned out like the cuff of a rolled-up sleeve. His whole face is distorted, turned inside out—he is crying loudly, rushing from someone at full speed—and the stamping of feet behind him . . .

The boy reminded me: Yes, U must be at school today, I must hurry. I ran to the nearest stairs to the underground.

In the doorway, someone, rushing past: "Not running! Trains aren't running today! There . . ."

I went down. Utter delirium. Glitter of faceted, crystal suns. Platform densely packed with heads. An empty, motionless train.

And in the silence—a voice. Hers. I could not see her, but I knew this firm, pliant voice like a striking whip—and somewhere, the sharp triangle of eyebrows raised to temples. . . .

I shouted, "Let me! Let me through! I must . . ."

But someone's fingers dug into my arms, my shoulders, like a vise, nailing me down. In the silence, the voice: "Run upstairs! They'll cure you, they'll stuff you full of rich, fat happiness, and, sated, you will doze off peacefully, snoring in perfect unison—don't you hear that mighty symphony of snores? Ridiculous people! They want to free you of every squirming, torturing, nagging question mark. And you are standing here and listening to me. Hurry upstairs, to the Great Operation! What is it to you if I stay here—alone? What is it to you if I don't want others to want for me, if I want to want myself—if I want the impossible. . . ."

Another voice—slow, heavy: "Ah! The impossible? That means running after your stupid fantasies, which wag their tails before your nose? No, we'll grab them by the tail, and crush them, and then . . ."

"And then gobble them up and snore—and there will have to be a new tail before your nose. They say the ancients had an animal they called an ass. To force it to go forward, ever forward, they would tie a carrot to the harness shaft before him, just where he could not reach it. And if he reached it and gobbled it down ..."

Suddenly the vise released me. I rushed to the middle, where she was speaking. But at that moment everybody surged, crushed together—there was a shout behind: "They're coming, they're coming here!" The light flared, went out—someone had cut the wire. An avalanche of bodies, screams, groans, heads, fingers. ...

I don't know how long we rolled so through the underground tube. At last, stairs, a dim light, growing lighter—and once more out in the street, fanlike, in all directions.

And now—alone. Wind, gray twilight—low, just overhead. On the wet glass of the pavement—deep, deep—the upside-down lights, walls, figures moving feet up. And the incredibly heavy roll in my hand—pulling me into the depths, to the very bottom.

Downstairs, at the table,—there was still no U, and her room was empty, dark.

I went up to my room, switched on the light. My temples throbbed in the tight circle of the hoop, I was still locked within the same circle: the table, on the table the white roll; bed, door, table, white roll ... In the room on the left the shades were down. On the right, over a book—a knobby bald head, the forehead a huge yellow parabola. The wrinkles on the forehead—a row of yellow, illegible lines. Sometimes our eyes would meet, and then I felt: they were about me, those yellow lines.

It happened exactly at 21. U came to me herself. Only one thing remains clear in my memory: I breathed so loudly that I heard my own breathing, and tried and tried to lower it—and could not.

She sat down, smoothed her unif on her knees. The pink-brown gills fluttered.

208

"Ah, my dear—so it is true that you were hurt? As soon as I learned—I immediately . . ."

The rod was before me on the table. I sprang up, breathing still more loudly. She heard it, halted in mid-sentence, and also, for some reason, stood up. I saw already that place on her head. . . . A sickening sweetness in my mouth. . . . My handkerchief—but it wasn't there; I spat on the floor.

The one behind the right wall—with yellow, intent wrinkles—about me. He must not see, it will be still more disgusting if he sees. . . . I pressed the button—what difference if I had no right to, it was all the same now—the shades fell.

She evidently understood, dashed to the door. But I anticipated her—and, breathing loudly, my eyes fixed every moment on that spot on her head . . .

"You . . . you've gone mad! Don't dare . . ." She backed away—sat down, or, rather, fell on the bed, thrust her folded hands between her knees, trembling. Tense as a spring, still holding her firmly with my eyes, I slowly stretched my hand to the table—only my hand moved—and seized the rod.

"I beg you! One day—only one day! Tomorrow— tomorrow I'll go and do everything . . ."

What was she talking about? I swung at her. . . .

And I consider that I killed her. Yes, you, my unknown readers, you have the right to call me a murderer. I know I would have brought the rod down on her head if suddenly she had not cried, "Please . . . for the sake . . . I agree—I . . . in a moment."

With shaking hands she pulled off her unif. The large, yellow, flabby body fell back on the bed. . . . And only now I understood: she thought I had lowered the shades . . . that I wanted . . .

This was so unexpected, so absurd, that I burst out laughing. At once the tigthly wound spring

209

within me cracked, my hand hung limp, the rod clanked on the floor. And I learned from my own experience that laughter was the most potent weapon: laughter can kill everything—even murder.

I sat at the table and laughed—a desperate, final laugh—and could see no way out of this preposterous situation. I don't know how it all would have ended if it had proceeded in a normal way—but suddenly a new, external component was added: the telephone rang.

I rushed, grasped the receiver. Perhaps it was she? But an unfamiliar voice said, "Just a moment."

A tormenting, endless hum. From a distance, a heavy tread, coming nearer, more resonant, more leaden. Then "D-503? Uh-uh . . . This is the Benefactor speaking. Report to me at once!"

Clink—the receiver was down—clink.

U still lay on the bed, eyes closed, gills spread wide in a smile. I gathered up her dress from the floor, flung it at her, and, through my teeth, "Here! Quick, quick!"

She raised herself on her elbow, her breasts swished sideways, eyes round, all of her waxen.

"What?"

"Just that. Well, hurry—get dressed!"

All doubled up into a knot, clutching her dress, her voice strangled. "Turn away. . . ."

I turned, leaned my forehead against the glass. Lights, figures, sparks trembled in the black wet mirror. No, it is I, the trembling is within me. . . . Why did He call me? Does He already know everything about her, about me, about everything?

U, dressed, was at the door. Two steps to her, and I squeezed her hands as though expecting to squeeze out everything I needed from those hands. "Listen . . . Her name—you know whom I mean—

did you name her? No? But only the truth—I must know ... I don't care—only the truth ..."

"No."

"No? But why—since you had gone there and reported ..."

Her lower lip was suddenly turned out, like that boy's—and from the cheeks, down the cheeks—drops ...

"Because I ... I was afraid that ... if I named her ... you might ... you would stop lov—... Oh, I can't—I couldn't have. ..."

I knew it was the truth. An absurd, ridiculous, human truth! I opened the door.

Thirty-sixth Entry

TOPICS: Blank Pages
The Christian God
About My Mother

It's strange—there seems to be a blank white page inside my head. I don't remember how I walked there, how I waited (I know I waited)—nothing, not a single sound, or face, or gesture. As if all the lines connecting me with the world were cut.

I recalled myself only when I stood before Him, and was terrified to raise my eyes: I saw only His huge, cast-iron hands upon His knees. These hands seemed to weigh down even Him, bending His knees. Slowly He moved His fingers. The face was somewhere high up, in a haze, and it seemed that His voice did not thunder, did not deafen me, was like an ordinary human voice only because it came to me from such a height.

"And so—you too? You, the Builder of the *Integral?* You, who were to have become the greatest of conquistadors? You, whose name was to initiate a new, magnificent chapter in the history of the One State. ... You?"

The blood rushed to my head, my cheeks. Again a blank page—nothing but the pulse in my temples, and the resonant voice above, but not a single word. It was only when He ceased to speak that I recovered. I saw: the hand moved with the weight of a hundred tons—crept slowly—and a finger pointed at me.

"Well? Why are you silent? Is this so, or is it not? An executioner?"

"It is so," I answered obediently. And then I clearly heard every word He spoke: 'Oh, well! You think I am afraid of this word? Have you ever tried to pull off its shell and see what is inside? I will show you. Remember: a blue hill, a cross, a crowd. Some—above, splashed with blood, are nailing a body to a cross; others—below, splashed with tears—are looking on. Does it not seem to you that the role of those above is the most difficult, the most important? If not for them, would this entire majestic tragedy have taken place? They were reviled by the ignorant crowd: but for that the author of the tragedy—God—should have rewarded them all the more generously. And what about the most merciful Christian God, slowly roasting in the fires of hell all who would not submit? Was He not an executioner? And was the number of those burned by the Christians on bonfires less than the number of burned Christians? Yet—you understand—this God was glorified for ages as the God of love. Absurd? No, on the contrary: it is testimony to the ineradicable wisdom of man, inscribed in blood. Even at that time— wild, shaggy—he understood: true, algebraic love of humanity is inevitably inhuman; and the inevitable mark of truth is—its cruelty. Just as the inevitable mark of fire is that it burns. Show me fire that does not burn. Well—argue with me, prove the contrary!"

How could I argue? How could I argue, when these were (formerly) my own ideas—except that I

213

had never been able to clothe them in such brilliant, impenetrable armor? I was silent. . . .

"If this means that you agree with me, then let us talk like adults, after the children have gone to bed: let us say it all, to the very end. I ask you: what did people—from their very infancy—pray for, dream about, long for? They longed for some one to tell them, once and for all, the meaning of happiness, and then to bind them to it with a chain. What are we doing now, if not this very thing? The ancient dream of paradise . . . Remember: those in paradise no longer know desires, no longer know pity or love. There are only the blessed, with their imaginations excised (this is the only reason why they are blessed) —angels, obedient slaves of God. . . . And now, at the very moment when we have already caught up with the dream, when we have seized it so (He clenched His hand: if it had held a stone, it would have squeezed juice out of it), when all that needed to be done was to skin the quarry and divide it into shares—at this very moment you—you . . ."

The cast-iron echoing voice suddenly broke off. I was red as a bar of iron on the anvil under the striking hammer. The hammer hung silently, and waiting for it was even more terrify . . .

Then, suddenly: "How old are you?"

"Thirty-two."

"And your naïveté is of someone half that age—someone of sixteen! Has it really never entered your head that they—we still don't know their names, but I am certain we shall learn them from you—that they needed you only as the Builder of the *Integral?* Only in order to use you as . . ."

"Don't! Don't!" I cried.

It was like holding up your hands and shouting it to a bullet: you still hear your ridiculous

"Don't," and the bullet has already gone through you, you are already writhing on the floor.

Yes, yes—the Builder of the *Integral* . . . Yes, yes . . . and all at once—the memory of U's raging face with quivering brick-red gills—that morning, when they both were in my room . . .

I clearly remember: I laughed, and raised my eyes. Before me sat a bald, Socratically bald, man, with tiny drops of sweat on his bald head.

How simple everything was. How majestically banal and ridiculously simple.

Laughter choked me, broke out in puffs. I covered my mouth with my hand and rushed out.

Stairs, wind, wet, jumping fragments of lights, faces—and, as I ran: No! To see her! Only once more—to see her!

And here again there is a blank white page. I can remember one thing only—feet. Not people—feet. Hundreds of feet falling from somewhere down on the pavement, stamping without rhythm, a heavy rain of feet. And a gay, mischievous song, and a shout—probably to me—"Hey, Hey! Come here, to us!"

Then—a deserted square, filled to the brim with dense wind. In the middle, a dim, heavy, dreadful mass—the Benefactor's Machine. And—such a strange, seemingly incongruous echo within me: a dazzling white pillow; on the pillow, a head, thrown back, with eyes half-closed; the sharp, sweet line of teeth . . . And all of this absurdly, terrifyingly connected with the Machine—I know how, but I still refuse to see, to name it aloud—I do not want to—no.

I shut my eyes and sat down on the stairs leading up to the Machine. It must have been raining. My face was wet. Somewhere in the distance, muffled cries. But no one hears me, no one hears me cry: Save me from this—save me!

If I had a mother, like the ancients: mine—yes, precisely—my mother. To whom I would be—not the Builder of the *Integral*, and not number D-503, and not a molecule of the One State, but a simple human being—a piece of herself, trampled, crushed, discarded. . . . And let me nail, or let me be nailed—perhaps it's all the same—but so that she would hear what no one else heard, so that her old woman's mouth, drawn together, wrinkled . . .

Thirty-seventh Entry

TOPICS: An Infusorian
End of the World
Her Room

In the dining room in the morning, my neighbor on the left said to me in a frightened whisper, "Why don't you eat! They're looking at you!"

With an enormous effort, I forced myself to smile. And felt it like a crack in my face: I smiled—the edges of the crack spread wider, hurting me more and more. . . .

Then, just as I picked up a tiny cube of food with my fork, the fork shook in my hand and clicked against the plate. And at that moment the tables, the walls, the dishes, the air itself—all shook and rang and clattered, and outside—an immense, round, iron roar, up to the sky—over heads, over buildings, slowly dying out far away in faint, small circles, like circles on the surface of water.

I saw faces instantly blanched, faded, mouths stopped in mid-motion, forks frozen in the air.

Then everything was thrown into confusion, slipped off the age-old tracks. Everybody jumped up (without singing the Hymn) —chewing without rhythm, swallowing hastily, choking, grasping at each other. "What is it? What happened? What?" And, like disorderly fragments of a once harmonious, great Machine, they poured down, to the elevators, the stairs: steps, thumping, parts of words—like pieces of a torn letter swept by the wind. ...

People were also pouring out of the other buildings, and in a minute the avenue was like a drop of water under a microscope: infusoria locked within the glasslike, transparent drop, rushing in wild confusion up, down, sideways.

"Ah-ah!" Someone's triumphant cry. Before me, the back of his neck, and a finger aimed at the sky—I remember with utmost clarity the yellowish-pink nail and at its base a white crescent, like the moon rising over the rim of the horizon. And, as if following a compass needle, hundreds of eyes turned up to the sky.

There, escaping from some invisible pursuit, clouds were flying, crushing, leaping over one another—and, shadowed by the clouds, dark aeros of the Guardians with black, suspended elephant trunks of observation tubes—and, still farther—in the west, something resembling ...

In the beginning, no one understood it. Even I, to whom (unfortunately) more had been revealed than to the rest, did not understand. It looked like an enormous swarm of black aeros: barely visible quick dots at an incredible height. Nearer and nearer; hoarse, guttural sounds from above—and finally, over our heads—birds. Their sharp, black, piercing, falling triangles filled the sky. The storm flung them down, they settled on cupolas, on roofs, on poles, on balconies.

"Ah-ah." The triumphant neck turned, and I saw that one, of the overhanging brow. But now the only thing remaining of his old self was the description; he had somehow emerged from under his eternal brow, and his face was overgrown with

218

bright clusters of rays, like hair—around the eyes, at the lips: he was smiling.

"Do you realize it?" he cried to me through the whistling of the wind, the wings, the cawing. "Do you realize?—the Wall, the Wall was blown up! You un-der-stand?"

Past us, somewhere in the background, flashing figures—heads stretched forward—running quickly inside, into the houses. In the middle of the street— a rapid, yet seemingly slow (because of their weight) avalanche of operated ones, marching westward.

Hairy clusters of rays at the lips, the eyes. I seized him by the hand. "Listen, where is she, where is I-330? Is she there, behind the Wall? Or . . . I must—you hear? At once, I cannot . . ."

"Here," he cried gaily, drunkenly—strong, yellow teeth . . . "She's here, in the city, in action. Oh-ho— we are acting!"

Who are we? Who am I?

Near him there were some fifty like him—out from under their dark brows, loud, gay, with strong teeth. Gulping the storm with open mouths, swinging seemingly innocuous electrocutors (where did they get them?), they also moved westward, behind the operated ones, but flanking them—by the parallel Avenue Forty-eight . . .

I tripped against tight, wind-woven cables and ran to her. What for? I don't know. I stumbled. Empty streets, an alien, wild city, an incessant, triumphant chorus of bird cries, the end of the world. Through the glass walls of some houses I saw (it etched itself in memory) male and female numbers copulating shamelessly—without even dropping the shades, without coupons, at midday . . .

A house—hers. A door gaping wide in confusion. Below, at the control table—no one. The elevator was stuck somewhere in the shaft. Panting, I ran up the endless stairs. A corridor. Quick—like wheel-spokes—figures on the doors: 320, 326, 330 ... I-330, here!

Already through the glass door I saw everything in the room—scattered, confused, crumpled. A chair turned over in haste, its four legs in the air, like a dead animal. The bed—pushed somehow absurdly sideways from the wall. On the floor—like trampled, fallen petals—a spray of pink coupons.

I bent down, picked up one, another, a third: all bore the number D-503. I was on each one, drops of me, molten, spilled over the brim. And this was all that remained ...

For some reason, it was impossible to leave them on the floor, to be trampled on. I gathered up another handful, put them on the table, smoothed them carefully, glanced at them, and ... laughed.

I had never known this before, but now I know it, and you know it: laughter can be of different colors. It is only an echo of a distant explosion within you. It may be festive—red, blue, and golden fireworks; or—torn fragments of a human body flying up. ...

An unfamiliar name flashed on a coupon. I do not remember the number, only the letter: F. I brushed all the coupons off the table, stepped on them—on myself—with my heel, like this, and went out. ...

For a long time, dumbly, I sat in the corridor near the door, waiting for something. Shuffling steps from the left. An old man: face like a punctured, empty, shrunken, creased balloon—with something transparent still dripping through the punctures, slowly trickling down. Slowly, dimly, I understood—tears. And only when the old man was already far, I recalled myself and cried out, "Wait—listen, do you know? Number I-330 ..."

The old man turned, waved his hand despairingly, and hobbled on. . . .

At dusk, I returned home. In the west, the sky contracted every second in a pale blue spasm. A dull, muffled roar came from there. The roofs were covered with black, charred pieces—birds.

I lay down on the bed—and like a heavy beast sleep weighed me down, stifled me. . . .

Thirty-eighth Entry

TOPICS : I don't know—perhaps only one:
A Discarded Cigarette

When I awakened, the brightness hurt my eyes. I closed them tightly. In my head—a strange, caustic, blue haze. Everything as in a fog. And through the fog: But I didn't turn on the light! How ...

I jumped up. At the table, her chin resting on her hand, sat I-330, looking at me with a wry smile. ...

I am writing on this table now. Those ten or fifteen minutes, brutally twisted into the tightest spring, are long past. And yet, it seems to me, the door has just swung shut behind her, and it's still possible to catch up with her, to seize her hands—and she may laugh and say ...

I-330 sat at the table. I rushed to her. "You, you! I was—I saw your room—I thought you . . ."

But in mid-word I tripped against the sharp, immobile spears of lashes. I stopped, remembering: this was how she looked at me that day, aboard the *Integral*. And yet I must now, in a single second, find a way of telling her—of making her believe—or else it will be never ...

"Listen to me—I must ... I must tell you ... everything. ... No, just a moment—I have to take a drink ..."

My mouth was dry as though lined with blotting paper. I tried to pour some water, and I couldn't. I put the glass down on the table and seized the pitcher with both hands.

Now I saw: the blue smoke was from her cigarette. She brought it to her lips, inhaled, greedily swallowed the smoke, as I the water, and said, "Don't. Be silent. It does not matter. You see, I came anyway. They are waiting for me below. And you want our last minutes to ..."

She flung the cigarette down on the floor, leaned backward with her whole body over the arm of the chair (the button was there, on the wall, and it was difficult to reach). And I remember how the chair tilted and two of its legs were lifted from the floor. Then the shades fell.

She came over, embraced me, hard. Her knees through her dress—the slow, tender, warm, all-enveloping poison ...

Then suddenly ... It sometimes happens that you have sunk completely into a sweet, warm dream—and suddenly you're stung by something, you start, and you are wide awake. ... So now: the trampled pink coupons on the floor in her room, and on one—the letter F, and some figures. ... They tangled within me into a single knot, and even now I don't know what the feeling was, but I crushed her so that she cried out with pain. ...

Another minute—of those ten or fifteen on the dazzling white pillow—her head thrown back with half-closed eyes; the sharp, sweet line of teeth. And all that time, the persistent, absurd, tormenting intimation of something that must not be ... that must not be remembered now. And I press her ever more tenderly, more cruelly—the blue spots from my fingers deeper, brighter. . . .

Without opening her eyes (I noticed this), she said, "I heard that you were at the Benefactor's yesterday. Is that true?"

"Yes, it is."

Then her eyes opened, wide—and I took pleasure in watching how rapidly her face paled, faded, disappeared: nothing but eyes.

I told her everything. Except—I don't know why . . . No, it isn't true, I know—except for one thing—the words He had spoken at the very end, that they had needed me only . . .

Gradually, like a photographic image in the developer, her face emerged: her cheeks, the white line of her teeth, her lips. She rose, went over to the mirrored closet door.

Again my mouth was dry. I poured myself some water, but it nauseated me. I put the glass back on the table and asked, "Is this what you have come for—you needed to find out?"

The sharp, mocking triangle of eyebrows raised to the temples looked at me from the mirror. She turned to say something to me, but said nothing.

There was no need. I knew.

Bid her good-by? I moved my—alien—feet, caught at the chair—it fell prone, dead, like the other one, in her room. Her lips were cold, as cold as, once upon a time, the floor here, near my bed.

And when she left, I sat down on the floor and bent down over her discarded cigarette.

I cannot write any more—I do not want to any more!

TOPIC : The End

All this was like the final grain of salt dropped into a saturated solution: rapidly, bristling like needles, the crystals began to form, congeal, solidify. And it was clear to me: all is decided—tomorrow morning *I shall do it*. It is the same as killing myself—but perhaps this is the only way to resurrection. For only what is killed can be resurrected.

In the west, the sky shuddered every second in a blue spasm. My head burned and hammered. I sat so all night, falling asleep only at seven in the morning, when the darkness was already drawn out, turning green, and I could see the bird-strewn roofs.

I awakened at ten—there had evidently been no bell today. A glass of water—last night's—stood on the table. I gulped it down greedily and ran out: I had to do it quickly, as quickly as I could.

The sky was empty, blue, all of it eaten away by the storm. Jagged corners of shadows, everything cut out of blue autumn air—thin—too fragile to be touched, or it will snap, be pulverized to flying glass dust. And the same within me: I must not think, I must not think, I must not think, or . . .

And I did not think. Perhaps I did not even see properly—merely registered. There, on the pavement, branches from somewhere, their leaves green, amber, crimson. Up above, crossing each other's paths, birds and aeros tossing this way and that. Here—heads, open mouths, arms waving branches. All this must have been shouting, cawing, buzzing. . . .

Then empty streets—as if swept clean by plague. I remember tripping on something unbearably soft, yielding, yet motionless. I bent down—a corpse. It lay on its back, its bent legs spread apart like a woman's. The face . . .

I recognized the thick, Negroid lips, which even now still seemed to spray me with laughter. With tightly shut eyes, he laughed into my face. A moment—I stepped across him and ran—because I could bear it no longer, I had to get it over with quickly, or else, I felt, I would snap, warp like an overloaded rail. . . .

Luckily, I was already just twenty steps away—here was the sign with golden letters—OFFICE OF THE GUARDIANS. On the threshold I stopped, took a deep gulp of air—as much as I could hold—and entered.

Inside, in the corridor, there was an endless queue of numbers, some with sheets of paper, others with thick notebooks in their hands. Slowly, they would move—a step, two—then stop again.

I rushed along the queue. My head was splitting, I grabbed people by the elbow, pleaded with them as a sick man pleads to hurry, to give him something that would end his torment in a single moment of sharpest pain.

A woman with a belt drawn tightly over her

unif, the bulging hemispheres of her rear end continually moving from side to side, as though she had eyes in them, snorted at me, "He has a belly-ache! Take him to the toilet—there, the second door on the right. . . ."

They laughed at me, and from this laughter something rose up in my throat, and in a moment I'd scream, or . . . or . . .

Suddenly, someone seized me by the elbow from behind. I turned: translucent, winglike ears. This time, though, they were not pink, as usual, but scarlet. His Adams's apple was jumping up and down in his throat—another second, and it would break the thin sheath of skin.

"Why are you here?" he asked, quickly boring into me.

I clutched at him. "Quick—let's go to your office . . . I must . . . immediately—about everything! It's good it will be you. . . . It may be terrible that it has to be you, but it is good, it's good. . . ."

He also knew *her*, and this made it still more agonizing for me, but perhaps he, too, would shudder when he heard, and then we would be killing her together; I would not be alone that dreadful last moment of my life. . . .

The door slammed shut. I remember: a piece of paper stuck to the door below and scraped against the floor while it was closing. Then a strange, airless silence covered us as though a glass bell had descended on the room. If he had said a single word—no matter which, even the most trivial—I would have burst out with everything at once. But he was silent.

And, straining till my ears hummed, I said, without looking up, "It seems to me I have always hated her, from the very first. I fought against . . . But no, no, don't believe me: I could and did not want to save myself, I wanted to perish—this was

227

more precious, more desirable than anything else. ... I mean, not perish, but so that she ... And even now, even now, when I know everything. .... You know—you know that I was summoned by the Benefactor?"

"Yes, I know."

"But the thing He told me ... You understand—it was as if ... as if the floor were to be pulled this moment from under you, and you, and all around you, all that's on this table—the paper, the ink—the ink would spurt, and everything—a shapeless blot ..."

"Go on, go on! But hurry. Others are waiting outside."

And then, breathless, confused—I told him everything I've written down here. About the real me, and the shaggy me, and what she told me that day about my hands—yes, that was when it all began ... And how I had not wanted to fulfill my duty, how I deceived myself, how she had gotten false medical certificates, and how the corrosion in me grew from day to day, and about the corridors below, and how—out there, beyond the Wall ...

All this in disconnected lumps and fragments—I panted, I lacked words. The crooked, doubly curved lips offered me the needed words with a dry grin—I nodded gratefully: Yes, Yes. ... And then—what did it mean?—then he was speaking for me, and I merely listened: "Yes, and then ... That's how it was, exactly, yes, yes!"

I felt my neck, around the collar, turning cold as if from ether, and I asked with difficulty, "But how—but you couldn't have known—not this ..."

His grin—silent—more and more crooked ... Then, "But, you know, there was something you've tried to keep from me. You named everyone you saw behind the Wall, but you've forgotten one. Do you deny it? Don't your remember—for a second—a flash—you saw ... me? Yes, yes, me."

A pause.

And suddenly, with lightning, shameless clarity, I knew: he—he was also one of them. ... And all of me, all of my pain, all that, in utter exhaustion, with a final effort, I had brought here, as if performing a great feat—all this was merely as ridiculous as the ancient anecdote about Abraham and Isaac. Abraham—in a cold sweat—has already lifted the knife over his son, over himself—when suddenly there is a voice from above: "Don't bother! I was only joking. ..."

Without tearing my eyes away from the increasingly crooked grin, I pressed my hands against the edge of the table and slowly, slowly rode away, together with my chair; then suddenly—as though gathering all of myself into an armful—I dashed out blindly, past cries, stairs, mouths.

I don't remember how I got downstairs. I found myself in one of the public toilets in an underground station. Above, everything was perishing, the greatest and most rational civilization in history was collapsing, but here, by someone's irony, all was as it had been—beautiful and still. And just to think that all of it was doomed, that grass would overgrow all of it, and only "myths" would remain. ...

I moaned aloud. And at that moment I felt someone gently stroking my shoulder.

It was my neighbor, who occupied the seat on my left. His forehead—an enormous bald parabola; on the forehead, yellow illegible lines of wrinkles. And those lines were about me.

"I understand you, I understand you very well," he said. "Nevertheless, you must calm yourself. Don't. All of this will return, it will inevitably return. The only important thing is that everyone must learn about my discovery. You are the first to hear it: according to my calculations, there is no infinity!"

I stared at him wildly.

"Yes, yes, I am telling you: there is no infinity. If the universe were infinite, then the mean density of matter in it should equal zero. And since it is not zero—we know that!—it means that the universe is finite; it is spherical in form, and the square of the cosmic radius, Y^2, equals the mean density multiplied by ... Now this is the only thing I need—to compute the digital coefficient, and then ... You understand: everything is finite, everything is simple, everything is calculable. And then we shall conquer philosophically—do you understand? And you, my dear sir, are disturbing me, you are not letting me complete my calculation, you are screaming. . . ."

I don't know what shook me more—his discovery, or his firmness at that apocalyptic hour. In his hands (it was only now that I noticed it) he had a notebook and a logarithmic table. And I realized that, even if everything should perish, it was my duty (to you, my unknown, beloved readers) to leave my notes in finished form.

I asked him for some paper—and it was there that these last lines were written ...

I was about to put the final period to these notes, just as the ancients put crosses over the pits where they had thrown their dead, when suddenly the pencil shook and dropped from my fingers.

"Listen." I tugged at my neighbor. "Just listen to me! You must—you must give me an answer: out there, where your finite universe ends! What is out there, beyond it?"

He had no time to answer. From above, down the stairs—the clatter of feet ...

Fortieth Entry

TOPICS: Facts
The Bell
I Am Certain

It is day. Bright. Barometer, 760.

Can it be true that I, D-503, have written these two hundred pages? Can it really be true that I once felt—or imagined that I felt—all this?

The handwriting is mine. And now—the same handwriting. But, fortunately, only the handwriting. No delirium, no absurd metaphors, no feelings: nothing but facts. Because I am well, I am entirely, absolutely well. I smile—I cannot help smiling: a kind of splinter was pulled out of my head, and the head feels light, empty. Or, to be more precise, not empty, but free of anything extraneous that might interfere with smiling (a smile is the normal state of a normal man).

The facts are as follows: that evening, my neighbor who had discovered the finiteness of the universe, I, and all who were with us were seized because we had no certificates to show we had been operated upon and were taken to the nearest auditorium (its number, familiar for some reason, was

231

112) . There we were tied to the tables and subjected to the Great Operation.

On the following day, I, D-503, went to the Benefactor and told him everything I knew about the enemies of happiness. How could it have seemed so difficult before? Incredible. The only explanation I can think of is my former sickness (the soul) .

In the evening of the same day, I sat (for the first time) at the same table with the Benefactor in the famous Gas Chamber. She was to testify in my presence. The woman smiled and was stubbornly silent. I noticed she had sharp and very white teeth, and that was pretty.

Then she was placed under the Bell. Her face became very white, and since her eyes are dark and large, it was very pretty. When they began to pump the air out of the Bell, she threw her head back, half closed her eyes; her lips were tightly shut—it reminded me of something. She looked at me, gripping hard the arms of the chair—looked until her eyes closed altogether. Then she was pulled out, quickly restored with the aid of electrodes, and placed once more under the Bell. This was repeated three times—and still she did not say a word. Others brought with that woman were more honest: many of them began to speak after the very first time. Tomorrow they will all ascend the stairs to the Benefactor's Machine.

This cannot be postponed, because in the western parts of the city there is still chaos, roaring, corpses, beasts, and—unfortunately—a considerable group of numbers who have betrayed Reason.

However, on the Fortieth cross-town avenue, we have succeeded in erecting a temporary barrier of high-voltage waves. And I hope that we shall conquer. More than that—I am certain we shall conquer. Because Reason must prevail.